Accelerated Reader
Level 5.1

Tell Me a Secret

HOLLY CUPALA

An Imprint of HarperCollinsPublishers

For
Ezri, my help
Lyra, my song
and Shiraz, my love

HarperTeen is an imprint of HarperCollins Publishers.
Lyrics from "Presumed Lost" by Melissa R. Kaplan copyright
© 1996 by Splashdown. Used by permission.

Tell Me a Secret
Text copyright © 2010 by Holly Cupala
All rights reserved. Printed in the United States of America.
No part of this book may be used or reproduced in any manner
whatsoever without written permission except in the case of brief
quotations embodied in critical articles and reviews. For information
address HarperCollins Children's Books, a division of HarperCollins
Publishers, 10 East 53rd Street, New York, NY 10022.
www.harperteen.com

Library of Congress Cataloging-in-Publication Data
Cupala, Holly.
Tell me a secret / by Holly Cupala. — 1st ed.
    p.   cm.
Summary: Seventeen-year-old Rand's unexpected pregnancy
leads her on a path to unravel the mystery of her sister's death and
face her own more hopeful future.
ISBN 978-0-06-176666-4 (trade bdg.)
[1. Sisters—Fiction. 2. Pregnancy—Fiction. 3. Secrets—
Fiction. 4. Family problems—Fiction. 5. Seattle (Wash.)—
Fiction.] I. Title.
PZ7.C91747Te 2010   2009035132
[Fic]—dc22   CIP
                                                            AC

Typography by Alison Klapthor
10 11 12 13 14   CG/RRDB   10 9 8 7 6 5 4 3 2 1

First Edition

Acknowledgments

I am indebted to many for their unflagging support:

To Edward Necarsulmer IV, who had me at "wow" and has been wowing me ever since, and to Catherine Onder and the HarperCollins team, whose talents glow with uncommon grace;

To the generous people at the Society of Children's Book Writers and Illustrators for the gift of a Work-In-Progress Grant;

To my panel of experts—Michelle Grandy, CNM; Kari Christie, MSW, LICSW; and Thom Johnson, Rocket Scientist—who helped me navigate possibilities, time, and space;

To Splashdown—Melissa Kaplan, Kasson Crooker, and Adam Buhler—for inspiration and use of lyrics from their song, "Presumed Lost";

To my writer friends and mentors: Molly Blaisdell, Annie Gage, Julie Reinhardt, Martha Brockenbrough, Sara Easterly, Mitali Perkins, Peggy King Anderson, Katherine Grace Bond, Judy Bodmer, Dawn Knight, Jet Harrington, Meg Lippert, Brenda Guiberson, Kathryn

Galbraith, Kirby Larson, Bonny Becker, Kathy Adler, Donna Bergman, Clare Meeker, and the readergirlz—Lorie Ann Grover, Dia Calhoun, Melissa Walker, and especially Justina Chen for opening one door and Janet Lee Carey for closing another;

To my parents, nieces Nellie and Molly, and family; to friends Amy, Deanna, Glynis, Pam, Alice, Kristine, Erika, Cathy, Claudia, the Crookers, the good people of Capitol Hill Pres, and the real BabyCenter girls—they know what is truth and what is fiction, but they will never tell.

Above all, I offer gratitude and love to my husband, daughter, and the memory of our dear Ezri—and to the Author and Finisher of our continuing story.

Tell Me
a Secret

One

It's tough, living in the shadow of a dead girl. It's like living at the foot of a mountain blocking out the sun, and no one ever thinks to say, "Damn, that mountain is big." Or, "Wonder what's on the other side?" It's just something we live with, so big we hardly notice it's there. Not even when it's crushing us under its terrible weight.

No one mentions my sister. If they do, it's mentioning her by omission, relief that I am nothing like *her*. I am the good sister. Thank God.

To speak of my sister . . . there's nothing more sacrilegious. Alexandra, Andra, Alex. Xanda—who was, and is, and is to come. To speak her name is my family's purest form of blasphemy.

To think of Xanda is to conjure up a person out of phase

with the rest of us. Gym socks and Mary Janes. Lipstick always slightly outside the lines, as if she were just the victim of a mad, messy kiss. Laddered stockings with dresses that were decidedly un-churchy. Sloppy in a way that was somehow repulsive and delectable at the same time. Repulsive to my parents. Delectable to me.

At ten, I was practicing her pout in the mirror. By twelve, I was trying on her clothes (in secret, of course), thrilled with the way her shorts hugged my cheeks and made my underpants seem obsolete. Xanda was seventeen. She didn't wear underpants.

One day she caught me in her boots and safety-pin dress, the one she had painstakingly assembled like rock-star chain mail. I was so scared I poked a pin through the end of my pinky. I imagined her taking off one of her stilettos and plunging it into my heart.

But Xanda didn't skewer me. Instead, she threw back her head and laughed a dazzling, tonsil-baring laugh, then smothered me in a hug. She had that sour, sharp smell, and I knew she had been with Andre—Andre, of the sultry voice and skin the shade of coffee with milk. *Café con leche*, as he put it. Sweet and dangerous. A bit of a con, said Andre. A bit of a letch, said my sister.

After she bandaged my finger, Xanda insisted I try on the matching safety-pin leg warmers. They hung like chains around my ankles. *Clump, clump, drag.* With a heavy grasp, she steered us both toward the full-length mirror on the back of her bedroom door. The metal of the safety pins shimmered down my straight, twelve-year-old hips. Xanda stood behind me, the glow of the bedroom window lighting up the pale chaos of her hair in a halo. She shimmered, too, but in a different kind of way. Her sheer white dress fluttered around her, a ghost trapped behind my chain-link figure. When she smiled, she looked like an unholy angel.

She studied my face with one eye closed, like an artist sizing up a canvas. "You know what?" she said. "I don't think you should be Mandy anymore."

"Should I be Miranda now?" I asked.

"No, I was thinking more like . . . Rand. Rand is so much cooler than Mandy. Kind of edgy. Don't you think?"

I tested the name in my mouth. Rand. Rand would wear a safety-pin dress. Rand could probably go without underpants now and then. Rand sounded almost like Xanda. I liked it.

"Do you want to know a secret?" I whispered to the sister in the mirror.

"Tell me," she whispered back. "Tell me, and I'll tell you one."

I cupped my hands around her ear. You never knew when our mother would turn a corner, shattering the most perfect moment with a well-placed shard of disapproval. Andre's scent lingered in Xanda's hair, filling my head and fueling my passionate announcement: "I want to be like you!"

Xanda staggered backward, the smile on her face slipping first into a grimace and then into a beaming hiccup. She threw her arms around me and rocked back and forth. Her body heaved with silent giggles until I nearly suffocated in her clutch. I laughed, too, at my own ridiculousness. It wasn't until she pulled away that I realized she was crying.

"You don't want to be like me." She swiped at the tears, smearing her left eye just enough to match her right. A bitter laugh gurgled up. "You'd be better off being like Mom than me."

The front door slammed—Mom returning from the church drama committee, or praying for Xanda's soul. The safety pins closed in on me like a thorny noose. My eyes met Xanda's in the mirror: panic in mine, resolve in hers. She pushed past me and out the door, where Mom saw her see-through dress and immediately began the usual tirade. *Dressed like a streetwalker . . . playing with fire . . . don't you see what you're doing to your life?*

I winced, knowing I could never stand up to the words my mother threw so easily at my sister. "That's just it, Mom," she countered. "It's my life, not yours."

Then it dawned on me: Xanda was buying me time. After wrestling with the pins, I escaped with only a few scratches through the secret passageway Dad had built between our bedrooms, her words burning in my heart. *Tell me, and I'll tell you one.*

Xanda never did tell me her secret, though I thought I

could guess. I could see it in her eyes the last time she left. I knew, from the suitcase bursting with her clothes found in Andre's car when they tried to escape Seattle forever.

"It was that boy," my mother told me the night she died. "It was that Andre's fault, for his drinking." And Dad's, for bringing him into our lives.

In the five years after Xanda died, each of my parents disappeared behind a locked door, NO UNAUTHORIZED ENTRY—Mom into drama and the prayer chain, Dad into his construction business. I was left to wonder, what role did Xanda fill that I could not? What secret did she keep? And what path could I take to find it?

Any choice could lead to something irrevocable, as my boyfriend, Kamran, would say. I had to tread carefully.

I first saw Kamran checking out my labyrinth drawings in the Elna Mead Junior Class Art Exhibition last February. A guy I'd never seen before hovered right next to the display glass, drinking in the lines of my mazes as though he were trying to navigate them.

He wasn't much taller than me, with metal-rimmed glasses, combat boots, casually holding a motorcycle helmet. He stood there at some point nearly every day, absorbing the images and making notes in a small notebook. I would find it odd if he wasn't so hot.

Essence was my spy and confidante, back when we were still friends. Before Delaney Pratt changed everything.

"Yup, he's still there," Essence said, plopping her books

down next to me in chem class. "Do you think he's a freak or something?"

"No," I said. "I think he's cute. I haven't seen him before. Do you think he's a transfer student? Ooh, maybe he's from Germany or Israel or something. He looks kind of Euro, you know?" And a little bit of *con leche*, I hoped.

"No idea. Maybe Eli knows."

Eli was Essence's new squeeze—actually, her first-ever squeeze. She had been spending an inordinate amount of time getting to know him and his tonsils, so I didn't see her much anymore outside of chem lab. They met in Drama, where Essence was honing her stage skills while I drifted deeper into preparing for art school—and checked out art-appreciating hotties.

Eli was not impressed with our sleuthing. "Are you blind? That's Kamran Ziyal. He's been around since second grade." Eli was haughty in that "I'm infinitely smarter than you" kind of way, which Essence thought was adorable. "Too cool to come down and mingle with the rest of us," he declared. "He's busy trying to get into aeronautics and astronautics at MIT." Perfect—a stone's throw away from my choice, Baird School of Fine Arts, in Boston.

I was too shy to say anything to this mysterious Kamran until the day I caught him holding a pencil and sheet of paper up to the glass—copying my work.

"Hey," I said, my outrage overcoming the tongue that had been tied up for weeks. "You can't copy that! It's mine!"

I sounded like a twelve-year-old, but I didn't care. If Mr. MIT Astronaut Man was going to copy my art, I wasn't above making a twelve-year-old stink.

He shifted his weight toward me, turning the full power of those olive eyes onto my face. I opened my mouth to shout something—anything—and he smiled a kind of cocky half-smile, knocking the rules of communication right out of my head.

White teeth . . . nice lips . . . eyelashes . . . I could no longer make sense of any of them. Except that they were talking to me. Well, the lips were talking to me. The eyes were looking at me in the same way they'd been looking at my art for the last month—searching for something beyond this dimension.

"I wasn't copying, I was making a sketch of it for the poem I've been writing about your art. I wanted to remember it."

The boy wrote poetry. About my art. I thought I was going to pass out.

"I'm studying hyperspace—you know, wormholes, which are kind of like labyrinths, only instead of traversing a landscape, they can traverse space and time, and possibly even an infinite number of galaxies. So I wanted to write about them. Your art inspired me."

Okay, make that hyperventilate, here in hyperspace, with the cute boy who writes poetry.

"Oh . . . oh," I stuttered. "So you write about wormholes. *Labyrinths*. I mean . . . labyrinths are my passion." They had been, ever since Xanda died.

He smiled even wider. "I can see that. I like labyrinths, too."

I was hooked, enough to keep checking for mystery-man Kamran lurking around my art and hopefully thinking about me as much as I was thinking about him.

When the display came down, I was afraid he would disappear.

Everything about last year seemed irrevocable now—the intersection of Kamran and me. Meeting Delaney. Losing Essence. The choices we made, the last time I saw them all.

I would not have chosen to spend the summer before my senior year working at Evergreen New Creation Camp teaching art. "After all," said my mother, "you can't be a teacher if you don't start acquiring some experience." *Make art, Mom, not teach art.* But it was pointless to remind her when she had already made up her mind. *Money in the bank,* Dad would say. You never knew when you'd need it.

It was as if they already knew what I'd done and had devised the perfect purgatory. They couldn't have chosen much worse than nine weeks at the church kiddie camp, eighty miles outside of Seattle. Nine weeks. Nine hundred kids. At least nine different behavioral disorders. And while I was painting crosses and rainbows and getting sick from the heat and collective prepubescent body odor, Kamran took classes and worked two jobs, Delaney jetted off to Amsterdam, and Essence would probably go to theater camp like she had every summer since fourth grade.

I returned home the week before school to life as usual in the Mathison house: Mom the drama queen, Dad the absentee, and me . . . a seventeen-year-old with too many secrets—and a mountain of my own, threatening to blow.

Two

Coming home after almost three months was like walking into someone else's house, all dressed up to look like ours. Same shiny wood floors speeding through the entry and into a bright, sunny kitchen; same white trim on white paneling; same whispered challenge to find a speck of dust or trace of actual humans living there—except for my own reflection in the mirror as soon as I crossed the threshold.

I looked at my face to see if anything had changed, if my secret was written there for anyone to read. But it wasn't. Grimy with camp dirt, bedraggled, tired—three sessions of summer campers left the only signs.

"Wait until you read my script, Mandy," my mom was saying as she pushed her way through the front door, dragging a summer's worth of my clothes on wheels. "I am so close—I was hoping to finish before you got home but ran out of time. You know how these things go. So much to do around here."

"I know," I said. It was all coming back to me. The notes. The scripts. The to-do lists. The never-ending cadre of people to impress.

All the way home, Mom had talked about her new script for this year's Christmas montage. *Almost finished, can't wait to get your opinion, will be the best one yet*, Mom went on. I wouldn't be seeing much of Dad—nothing new about that. The summer remodeling season wasn't over, then there would be the interior remodeling season, then set-building season, then the winter remodeling season. As if I needed an explanation after years of Dad never being home. I kept waiting for some sign of quiet rebellion, some indication he might one day break free and boogie. Either that, or ditch us for good.

"And the best part," she continued, brushing the hair out of my face and then wiping her hands on her skirt, "is what I've been writing for you—" A pause, for maximum effect. "—the *starring role*."

Once, there was a time when I might have been thrilled to hear those words spoken to me and not to my sister. We each had our parts to play in the perfect family drama: Mom, the director; Xanda, the actor; Dad, the builder; me, the backdrop. I had painted more sets than I could remember—living rooms, war zones, hospital corridors. Only once had I acted in one of Mom's plays—the year Xanda died.

"God, Mom, you don't have to force everybody into your lame-ass play," Xanda had said when Mom announced I would be the daughter of a traumatized soldier, the lead role originally meant for Xanda. Onstage, she could be the kind of daughter my mom wanted—the kind I already was, if only my parents would notice. But this year, Xanda refused the part.

"I'm not forcing you," Mom said. "I was asking Mandy."

"So you're forcing Rand instead. Do you even realize what a control freak you are?"

I stood there, trying to shift myself into part of the wall. They were like the angel and the devil, arguing over my soul. Good Mandy, Bad Rand. Or was it Bad Mandy, Good Rand?

"Mandy," said Mom, her teeth clenched as the word pried its way out. "I'm not forcing you, am I?" The question uncloaked me.

Xanda turned to me expectantly. "Well?" she demanded. "Do *you* want to be in the show?"

"I—I guess so."

Mom looked smug. Xanda looked utterly defeated. I felt like a traitor.

"Congratulations," Xanda sniped. "It looks like you've successfully created your own puppet government."

It didn't occur to me until much later that the role Mom offered had never been about me—only about getting to Xanda. I wondered what my mom had in mind now.

I smiled wearily. "Thanks, Mom. I'll be upstairs."

"You must be exhausted from the trip. Take a shower first though, huh? I just washed everything." She rolled my suitcase down the hall with two fingers, checking the floor for skid marks as she went.

I could hear her unzipping and sorting as I climbed the stairs, the squishy carpet familiar under my feet. I passed frame after frame of my drawings and paintings—all labyrinths. The same labyrinths that had brought Kamran and me together.

After the junior class art exhibit came down, a note tumbled out of my locker, written in tiny staccato handwriting: *Meet me under the plum tree.*

I read the note over and over, floating through the rest of my classes like plum blossoms. When the last bell rang, I found Kamran there, his helmet in one hand and a second one in the other, motorcycle standing by.

"I have a surprise for you. Hop on." Before I had a chance to ask where we were going, he fitted the helmet onto my head and slung on his own, then strapped our bags to the back. He mounted the bike and I wrapped myself around him, drinking in his musky smell with the faintest hint of sour-sweet.

As we wound our way through the streets, I couldn't stop thinking about my body against his or the warmth I felt through every layer. We crested Seattle's Capitol Hill neighborhood, where the past met the present in a violent tumble of brownstones and mansions, transients and transplants, infinite varieties of colors and art and self-expression. We nearly collided with pedestrians, odors exotic and taboo, and a thousand visual feasts.

"That's my parents' restaurant," he shouted, pointing to Café Shiraz, a hole-in-the-wall place with cinnamon and garlic scents emanating from the open door.

"Is that where we're going?"

"Later, maybe."

"Where, then?"

He grasped my hand with his nimble and smooth one. "Ask no questions, I tell no lies."

Commercial buildings blurred into brick apartments then towering evergreens near Cornish College of the Arts. He turned into the campus parking lot and led me through the heavy doors and stained glass to the current art exhibit: Travels through Space and Time.

Later, over kebabs and hummus and his mom's famous stuffed figs, we talked about light sources and vanishing points, MIT and Baird. He told me about his parents leaving everything to come here and start a restaurant, I told him about my parents disappearing into their work. I asked about physics. He asked about art. I stopped short of telling him about Xanda.

The office and basement were lit when we pulled up to my house—each of my parents in separate domains. Kamran and I sat on the curb under the rhododendrons, exactly the place where Andre parked his green Impala and Xanda disappeared into the night. We watched the sky turn from gray-gold to gray-plum, an echo of the paintings we'd seen at Cornish as we wandered the corridors, hand in hand. He was so close, I could feel the roughness of his jacket brushing up against my skin.

"So you never told me about your poetry."

"Ah, right." He grinned. "You mean when I was copying your artwork."

"Yes, as a matter of fact. So where is this so-called poem, inspired by my labyrinths?"

"Oh, that." He ran his fingers through rumpled hair, olive eyes squinting through dark, dark lashes. "You don't really want to see that."

"Oh, but I do." I felt out of my depth. Xanda would have pulled him close, felt the skin under his T-shirt, his waistband . . . for me, it was enough to be touching his sleeve.

He rummaged through a folder in his pack for a sheet of graph paper swirled over with that same tight handwriting. Sentences began in one corner and spread out like branches in a tree.

He held it aloft. "I don't know if I want you to see this— it's not actually a poem. Well, sort of. It's more like . . . strings of possibility." He sat down next to me, tracing his finger over the lines. "It's all the things that could bring a person to this point—"

"A person?"

"W-well, two people." Leaning over his shoulder, I caught only fragments: *She follows a path, a labyrinth . . . A landscape of mystery beneath her lines . . . A girl seeking shadows, past and future . . . What secret she seeks, unfolding lies . . .*

The sentences curled away from each other until I reached the top, the one that nearly stretched off the page: *. . . paths cross, time stops . . . then she and I would meet.*

Those sentences uncloaked me, the same way I felt when he lost himself in my mazes—like he already knew me. The thought both excited and terrified.

"To what point?" I asked, my voice unsteady. I could almost taste the figs lingering on his breath.

Then our lips met in our own mad, messy kiss, tender and fruity, pomegranate fireworks, his hands cupping my face and mine warm under his jacket, noses bumping and chins tilting until he pulled away, the two of us existing in a moment of perfection.

It was then that I knew I could tell him anything—about Xanda, the labyrinths. Someday I might even tell him about Andre.

Need to talk, Kamran's text had said. We'd barely spoken since I left in July, only a few clipped conversations and a backlog of unanswered messages—his and mine. I would have to tell him when I saw him. It would be his secret, too.

I shut myself in the bathroom. Stripping down had become a ritual at camp: hoping, checking, nothing. Delaney once said, "I don't worry too much if I only miss one." What if I'd missed two?

If it doesn't happen today, I thought, *I'll take a test.* But I'd have to see Kamran first. *Be wrong.*

Downstairs, my mom typed away on her laptop. ". . . Then the narrator, he'll be telling the backstory at this point, drumming up sympathy for the grand finale, the final moment when she reveals . . . oh, yes!" The sound of her whispering lines had exactly the same effect as a cheese grater on the back of my neck.

"Mom, can I use the car? I've gotta run some errands." Kamran would probably be at Big Boss now, or at his parents' restaurant.

"Okay, honey," she said distractedly. "Pick up a new toothbrush, will you? After two months at camp, yours is probably disgusting."

"Sure." The drugstore was already on my list.

"Oh, I forgot to mention—Delaney called," Mom sang as I reached the front door. "Back from her trip to Amsterdam?" She sure did like that Delaney girl. I would have to call her when I got back.

A half hour later, I steered around the massive Big Boss parking lot. A woman with a toddler rolled a cart piled high with diapers to an SUV while the car in front of me flipped on a blinker.

"Come on," I muttered, swinging wide with the Lexus.

That's when I saw him, looking not quite like himself in the red Big Boss vest and chasing down stray shopping carts, but entirely like the person whose body and soul had touched mine. I didn't even realize how much I'd missed him until now.

Only he wasn't alone.

He was with her. Delaney. Wearing a matching vest, hips

peeking out over her jeans as she slapped him on the butt.

The ground started sliding out from under me.

He laughed.

Collided a cart into hers.

Sent everything reeling, fissures cracking until I could no longer stand the pressure of my body, certain to implode at any moment.

I peeled out of the parking lot before either of them could spot me. There was a drugstore to find, a toothbrush to buy.

Not to mention a pregnancy test.

Three

Things could have been different if Delaney had chosen Brielle Peterson to show her around school last spring instead of me.

She landed in my first-period class in the empty seat next to me, a left-handed desk relegated to the back corner of the room. While the teacher droned on about world events and our role in them, I decorated my notes with an epic, convoluted network of lines and swirls.

"Psst." The new girl leaned over her desk to get a closer look. "What are you drawing?"

"Just . . . drawing," I mumbled. In fact, I was trying to remember the exact shape of the poem Kamran had shown me, the words curling from one branch to the next. She sat back again, scrutinizing her iPhone.

I'd heard about Delaney Pratt. Getting the boot from View Ridge Prep gave her instant mystique, especially at Elna Mead, home to a small army of punkalikes who were collectively spellbound by her hoarse laugh, street style, and ability to attract the attention of any straight male in the vicinity. Rumors swirled around her. Her dad was a Boeing exec, so whatever she'd done to get kicked out had to be huge.

When the bell rang, the teacher reached out for Brielle, junior-class president and leader of tomorrow. Delaney stood next to me, her hair falling in ripples over a shredded silk jacket, coiling around her limbs like nubby snakes. Something about her seemed terribly, wonderfully familiar.

The rest of the class scurried out the door while Brielle sized her up. As I gathered my book and papers, Brielle was saying, "Sure, I'd be happy to show her around."

Delaney's footsteps slowed. "Oh, thanks, but I already found someone to give me the tour." To me, she whispered, "What's your name again?"

"Rand." The teacher shrugged. Brielle rolled her eyes and stalked out.

"God, *thank you*." Delaney was rifling through her over-sized bag as we walked out together.

"So, um, I guess I can show you to your next class. Do you have a list?"

She found her keys next to a pack of Marlboros and put a cigarette behind her ear and the keys between her teeth. "Not likely," she muttered. She started toward the parking lot as the last of the students trickled into their classrooms, leaving me standing in the hall. "Coming?"

Essence would be waiting in chem but would forget all about me once she landed in drama with Eli. Kamran would be waiting for me after the last bell rang.

"Sure," I said, just before I caught up.

We wound our way around Lake Washington Boulevard in Delaney's Audi through a corridor of eight-foot laurels. A few sweeping estates spilled down the hill to the edge of the lake, just the sort of property my mom would have traded an eye for. Delaney's dad owned one of them.

In the granite-and-steel kitchen, Delaney poured herself a drink. She took one look at me and laughed. "If you think this is wild, you should meet my big brother, Dylan. He throws the most outrageous Halloween parties—come October, I'll take you. It'll crack open your universe." She took a gulp of her milky amber concoction. "Want some?"

"Won't your dad notice?"

She snorted. "I'd have to throw myself off a bridge for my dad to notice."

I knew exactly what she meant.

After my trip to Big Boss, I couldn't face my mom alone. I couldn't face anyone. I drove around numbly until I found a random drugstore to buy the test. And, of course, the toothbrush. But no amount of brushing could scrub away the hurt and panic I was feeling.

Kamran called twice that week, but I didn't trust myself to talk to him. Not now.

When I got home from the drug store, I'd hidden the test in the secret passage between Xanda's and my rooms. No one would look for it there.

What if he was only calling to break up with me? Telling him now would be like playing a trump card but losing the game. He had to *want* to fly away with me, like Andre did with Xanda. I could tell him then. I would take the test and we could figure out what to do together.

After his third message, I called back.

"You're home." Just hearing the crack in his voice threatened to break my resolve.

My throat caught with the words I wanted to say. *I miss you.* And I drew a breath to say them when he cut in.

"I need to talk to you . . . " He trailed off as a girl's laughter crackled in the background.

"Who's that?" I asked, trying to sound casual.

"I'm at work." Static whirled like a wind tunnel. "Hey, I can't really talk now. I'm trying to cram in hours before Monday. But I can call you later, or—"

Another voice muttered in the background, something starting with "Dude . . ."

"I need to talk to you, too. When can I see you?"

Kamran came back on the line. "A bunch of us are going to Chop Suey tonight."

"A bunch of us?"

"Yeah. Me, Delaney . . ."

"Delaney? Back from Amsterdam?"

"Yeah. About that . . ."

I knew all about that. While I finger painted and kept middle graders from sneaking off into the woods, Kamran spent the summer loading family reunion–sized bags of pretzels and motor oil with Delaney. Maybe he was wooing her with descriptions of the space-time continuum. Maybe she had caught him in the sphinx's gaze of her perfect chest. Maybe I should stop before I drove myself crazy.

". . . she didn't go to Amsterdam."

"Really."

"Her dad found out about us crashing at his cabin, so he canceled her trip, made her get a job—"

"That's what she said?" I felt myself shaking. "And neither one of you told me?"

Pause. "Wait a second. Why are you getting all worried about this?"

"Maybe because you didn't mention it?"

"I didn't mention it because . . . " He stopped himself. "You're right. I should have said something. I figured Delaney would have told you."

I knew what he would say—I was being insecure. Why did I worry so much? What did I think Delaney had that I didn't? Wasn't she supposed to be my friend?

"You don't even *know* her," I said hoarsely. Maybe I didn't either.

"You don't have to come tonight," he said. "I just thought . . ." The static went quiet again until I could hear the sound of his breath.

"Okay," I said. "I'll see you there."

Four

When Delaney picked me up to go to Chop Suey, she wasn't alone.

"You remember Chloe, right? From the French crowd?" I remembered Chloe, the quiet one who always seemed to be turning up next to someone, the serial sidekick. She sat in the front seat of Delaney's Audi. Since when were we hanging out with Chloe?

"Who's meeting us again?" I asked as I climbed into the backseat.

Delaney turned around and grinned. "Just us and Milo and"—she added in a sultry voice—"lover-man Kamran." Chloe giggled.

I felt my face burning. Did Kamran tell her? Maybe while

they were stocking the condom shelf at Big Boss? I touched the test in the bottom of my purse, still there waiting for me.

"And maybe Dylan, if he's around." Dylan, Delaney's infamous older brother, managed Chop Suey. He would let us in for shows and stuff, as long as we laid low and didn't try to get drinks. We didn't need them, anyway—Delaney always brought her own. I'd seen Dylan before but never actually met him. I'd even been to his house.

"You didn't invite Essence, did you?"

"Of course not." A year ago, it would have been me and Essence going out, or more likely hunkering down with cheese puffs, salsa, and *Into the Woods*. A year ago, I could have told Essence the truth. Now I couldn't even ask Delaney about Amsterdam.

She sped around the network of streets, chattering with Chloe, until we reached the Capitol Hill neighborhood. It was awkward, with Chloe there. She had one history with Delaney, I had another. I shifted in my seat, tugging at the bra which had suddenly become too tight.

"So," I said slowly, "Kamran told me about Amsterdam."

"Didn't I tell you?" Delaney snorted. "My dad found out about our party at the cabin and canceled the trip. It sucked—I had to work the whole summer. It would have been so much more fun if you were here." Chloe nodded, which both comforted and annoyed me.

A tiny constriction in my body relaxed.

I wanted to believe her. I did believe her. I just wanted

everything to go back to the way it was.

Outside the club, the guys were waiting. Delaney's party buddy, Milo, was half class clown and half class pothead; everybody liked him for one reason or another.

Then there was Kamran. The same messy, dark hair and olive-colored eyes . . . but different, somehow, like that night three months ago had never happened. His clothes were different—black and rumpled, like he had borrowed them from someone else. When I saw him, I couldn't even look him in the eye, I was trembling so much. Had he missed me as much as I'd missed him? Did he think about what had happened at the cabin as much as I did?

Then he smiled his beautiful smile, and I wondered if all of my worries had been for nothing. He held out his arm for me to tuck myself under, enveloping me into a hug.

"Are you okay?" he murmured into my ear.

"I'm just glad to see you." I squeezed, smelling the scent of lingering pomegranates.

"I'm sorry we didn't talk much. I've been working a lot." And then came the pat. Like a friend hug. *Pat, pat, pat* on my back, then release.

Delaney led the way into the booming club. Dylan or not, she would have made it in. She flirted with the bouncer, holding his eye contact as the rest of us trickled through. When Kamran passed, Delaney smacked him lightly on the shoulder. "You look smokin', brotha!" Kamran gave her a friendly jab, leaving me the last one out in the chill night air.

A wall of smoke and live bass hit me. Delaney lit one up, exhaling a lazy cloud. Chloe followed suit, and even she looked mysterious in the half-light of the club.

Kamran settled behind me, close but not too close. A vast gap had come between us in time and space. I wasn't sure how to cross it. "Miranda," he said. He never called me Mandy or Rand, always Miranda. "It's good to see you. You look pretty."

Did he have as much to say to me as I did to him? And how would I tell him?

"You said we need to talk."

His face darkened. "Yeah, but not right now. Too loud to talk here anyway."

He wrapped his arms around my ribs. I winced at the swelling in my chest and pulled away. "Okay, but we haven't even seen each other since . . . I mean, I want to spend time with you." *I want things to go back.*

"We're spending time together now, right?" He smiled. "You're so serious about everything, Miranda." I followed his gaze out to the dance floor, where Delaney's laughter wafted over the music. "Why can't you be more like Delaney? Lighten up. Have a little confidence in yourself."

"Right," I said. "Confidence. No problem." A little confidence, coming right up.

They all got sodas, and Delaney reached into her bag for a flask. I got orange juice. Anything bubbly would make me hurl.

"OJ and rum?" Delaney asked.

"I heard it was good."

Delaney shrugged. I flipped the flask and pretended to pour. Nobody noticed my thumb over the opening.

"Is your brother here?"

"Dylan? Nah. They said he cut out early. So he can't get in trouble for us being here—too bad. I think you'd like him."

The melody was intoxicating. Delaney snaked her way around the dance floor, and the rest of us followed in her wake. We had heard this band Gravity Echo before, a blend of indie electronic and a mournful exotic thread winding its way through the beat. Delaney shimmered like a mythical creature, her top reflecting the black lights and silhouetting her ribs and shoulders. She undulated to the beat. Next to her, my dancing would be the old middle-school step-touch. I imagined myself as a belly dancer caught in the music, shushing the idea away.

A ball of pain settled in my stomach, and my heart picked up. This was supposed to be my deadline—by the time I saw him—but the cramp gave me hope. "Be right back," I said to no one in particular.

The band's tunes beat against the walls of the bathroom, echoing the pounding in my head. My white patch of cotton panty blinked up at me in the black light.

Somewhere, I had taken a wrong turn and landed in the wrong life. Any moment I would find my way back. With any luck, I wouldn't have to wear this bra when I got there.

If nothing happens by the time school starts, I'll take the test then. Two more days.

I teetered out of the bathroom and headed toward the dance floor, trying to remember exactly when I would normally get tipsy. "Heeey," I practiced, lurching to the left. But the act dropped the second Delaney sidled up to Kamran. The dull ache in the pit of my stomach became a burn.

Red lights flashed over the crowd, and I could see her wiry frame shadowed by his taller one. Both of them had their hands in the air, her backside swaying against him. They parted, laughing, neither one of them seeing me on the sidelines. It was nothing, Kamran would say. They were playing around. Still, it should have been my backside.

Delaney caught my gaze and put her hand over her mouth in an embarrassed giggle. She sashayed over and crushed me in a hug. I could smell the rum and smoke on her breath. *I will not throw up here.*

"Sssno big deal!" she said, giggling. She hugged me harder, and I bit my lip. "I just wanted you to know, Rand, that you— you are my best friend. You and Chloe are my best friends in the whole world, you know that? You and Chloe and Kamran. I love you guys. You're all the best. Oh yeah, and Milo's okay, too," she said, spotting him dancing close to us. He smiled a lazy Milo smile and nodded his head when she draped herself around his neck and swayed to the curling beat of the music. Chloe, who had been dancing with him, caught my gaze. A flicker passed between us, then it was gone.

We always stayed at Delaney's dad's house when we went out—he wouldn't think twice about us coming in smelling like drunken ashtrays. Not that he was a bad parent—he just exhibited an unusual amount of disinterest in his daughter's nocturnal activities. None of us could argue with that.

We parted ways with the boys at the club, but not before they gave each of us a good-bye hug and Kamran put his lips to my forehead, a warm spark. But nothing compared to the lightning conducted through my spine when Kamran wrapped his arms around Delaney and dipped—closeness cultivated by weeks of togetherness at Big Boss.

On the way to Delaney's, we got into the "poor me" routine. This was our game, mine and Essence's, the one I made up to tease her about her never-ending stream of complaints. It was annoying, but at least she could laugh at herself. Never mind the pang of guilt I felt playing it with Delaney and now Chloe.

Delaney started: "I am so drunk, I am going to be completely sick all over the floor when I get home and my dad might finally kill me, if I haven't already died. Poor me!"

Chloe and I echoed, "Poor Delaney!"

Next, Chloe: "Nobody danced with me all night. Or at least, nobody cute. Just some dorky guy with a boy band T-shirt. Oh, and Milo. Poor me!"

"Poor Chloe!"

Then me.

I could say any number of things.

Like, "I miss my sister."

Or, "My best friend is moving in on my boyfriend."

Or the worst: "I haven't had a period in two months, and I'm scared out of my mind."

Delaney and Chloe were waiting.

Finally, I said, "My bra is too tight and my head is killing me. Poor me."

Five

Two days later, summer officially ended and I started life as a senior at Elna Mead High School. Kamran was taking AP Virtually Everything—calculus, computer science, physics, econ, U.S. history, and the English class we shared. I had AP art plus a couple of classes with Delaney. She had French with Chloe, where they learned to conspire in not one but two languages. Essence and I didn't cross paths at all. But with two thousand students, five hundred seniors, eighty classrooms, ten bathrooms . . . I was bound to run into her sooner or later.

Returning to these corridors after a whole summer had the same effect as coming home—displacement, like I was walking around in someone else's life. All day my mind had been traveling through timelines, possible outcomes. *Yes. No.* If no, then nothing would change. If yes, then another set of choices would branch out before me.

Posters lined the bulletin boards, advertising various activities and clubs. Online Gamers. Geography Club. Mock Trials. THE WINTER BALL COMMITTEE NEEDS YOU!

Right outside the theater hung a flyer for this year's musical tryouts: *Guys and Dolls*, Essence's favorite show. She knew every one of Adelaide's songs. *I* knew every one of Adelaide's songs, after she made me listen to the Broadway recording a hundred and fifty times. If I wanted to avoid Essence, all I had to do was stay away from the theater. She would know just by looking at me that something was wrong—ten years of friendship couldn't disappear that easily.

The test rattled in the bottom of my satchel. There was no way I could take it at home—not with my mother waiting to zap rebellion like bacteria. What would she do if she found out?

She wouldn't. The consequences were too horrible to imagine.

I was so wired that I didn't even notice Kamran hovering by my locker. He wore beat-up jeans and a hoodie with his hair tousled, a new and unfamiliar version of him.

"Miranda," he said. "You're off in space."

His smile made me flicker. *I could tell him now, before I even take the test.*

Kamran balanced two jobs, AP classes, homework, practice tests, spent every lunch period in the library, all to fulfill his dream—which may or may not include me. If I told him, what would he do?

If I haven't gotten it by art class.

"Yeah, just thinking about classes and stuff. How I'm going to fit everything in."

It had to be a mistake. Any second my body would return from its trip through hormonal haywire and the hall would quit spinning. I reached out for Kamran's arm.

"You okay?" he asked. Of course he was concerned. Because before the cabin trip, before he met Delaney, we had a deep, tangled connection. Was it possible to go back?

"We should hang out later," I said. "I've got . . . we haven't really had a chance to be together since . . ."

"Yeah, about that—I can't meet after school today. I'm studying to retake the SATs, plus I've been trying to hook up with this MIT graduate who does student interviews . . ." He trailed off. "But you're right, we should hang out. We haven't really had a chance to talk all summer."

I said nothing, but my disappointment must have shown on my face. "What about lunch? School just started—you can't have homework yet?"

"Aren't you going to hang out with Delaney?"

That's how it had been all last spring—my life divided into two separate trajectories: getting to know Kamran and spiraling further into a friendship with Delaney.

With Kamran, I had my own *con leche*. When he wasn't working one of his jobs or studying for one of the many entrance exams for MIT, we explored Seattle together, talking about time and space and possibilities, where wormholes and labyrinths collide. I told him about Xanda, but never about the way she died. It was too personal, too secret. *It was that Andre,* even though I didn't want it to be. Afterward, sitting under the rhododendrons, I would taste the fruit on his lips and the spice in his skin.

With Delaney, I became more than just an actor in someone else's script, the good daughter holding the weight of the family. Delaney led the way as my sister would have. She broke through closed doors into impenetrable circles, while Essence slipped further into my past. Any attempt to reconcile them resulted in a paradox—Essence the old friend, Delaney the new, with the old me and the new wrestling for control.

All this time, Delaney and Kamran never met. Somehow I knew if they crossed, my future would never be the same. And they didn't, until that night at the beginning of July, after school got out and we were all going out to party at Delaney's cabin, and Delaney pestered me about bringing along "that hottie," and Kamran accused me of shutting him out. In the end, I had no choice but to let the two halves of my life meet.

Everything changed that night.

Then a few days later, my parents packed me up for nine weeks at the kiddie camp, just like nothing had happened.

Delaney's ears must have been burning at the sound of her name—she came out of nowhere to pounce on Kamran and me at my locker. "So where are we going for lunch? Broadway

Grill? Bauhaus?" A slow grin spread across her face. "Café Shiraz?"

I glanced at Kamran. Had he taken her to his parents' restaurant or just told her about it?

"I can't—gotta study."

"During lunch period?" She turned to me. "Is that where you were hiding him all last year?"

Kamran laughed, showing off the tiny gap between his teeth and looking like he'd get a perfect score on a purity test. People like Delaney, like my sister, could do anything, say anything, and everyone still loved them. People like me just looked paranoid.

"Fine, then. I guess I'll see ya later," she said to no one in particular, sauntering away and disappearing into the stream.

I could hardly wait for my last period art class.

AP art was like coming back into myself, in a room I knew well. The bank of windows, paint-splattered sinks, drawers of possibilities, all of it seemed to sigh that yes, I belonged here. I found a seat by the window, nodding at familiar faces.

Our teacher, Mrs. Crooker, had a legendary personality at Elna Mead. There were the fat years and the lean years. In the fat years, she was in an excellent mood, letting us do whatever we wanted and usually working on some wild, colorful thing herself. In the lean years, she subsisted on diet sodas and 800 calories a day and morphed into a grouchy tyrant. In the lean years, she had patience as long as an oil pastel and gave assignments involving rigid architectural perspective and golden means. No cubism or impressionism in the lean years. My labyrinths barely slid under the radar as a loving tribute to Escher and da Vinci.

Thankfully, this was a fat year. She was already munching cheerfully on a package of molasses cookies.

Our first assignment was to create a double-sided collage of ourselves—one side our external selves, the other our secret, inner lives. "I want you to reach deep and come up with something fresh. It doesn't have to be good. I want it to be true. Have fun with it."

"No labyrinths this year," Mrs. Crooker said as she swept past me in a tiered cotton skirt. "I picked this assignment especially for you."

She proceeded to dump a shoebox full of magazine clippings, photocopies, engravings, fabric swatches, and handmade paper onto a table in the center of the room. "Have at it."

Students got up tentatively at first, then faster as they realized their true selves might be lurking somewhere in that pile of scraps. I held back, waiting, until a tiny black-and-white engraving of a medieval pregnant woman fluttered to the floor—the cap binding her hair in strange contrast to the way she gently held her belly.

There was no way I would be taking that piece.

Instead, I grabbed my stuff and dashed to the front desk.

"Somewhere to go?" The last of the molasses cookie popped

into Mrs. Crooker's mouth while she thumbed through her sketchbook, and I suddenly realized I was starving. Again.

"I'm not feeling so good. Could I get a hall pass?"

Her eyes never strayed from the book as she handed me a pass. "I want you to do this assignment at some point, Rand. You're not going to get away from faces this year."

I shrugged and made tracks for the nearest bathroom.

My hands trembled as I opened the package, so much that I almost dropped it onto the tiny beige floor tiles. I stripped the foil down to just the white plastic stick.

Place the absorbent tip in your urine stream for five seconds only, commanded the instructions. *One. Two. Three. Four. Five.*

After two perilous minutes, I peered at the little window. One pinkish-purple line was strong. I looked closer for a second line—so faint it seemed to shadow the first. I read the directions again, to be sure. *Lines may not be the same strength of color,* it taunted. *Over 99% accurate,* proclaimed the bold letters. And as I watched, the line darkened to a grim pink. My stomach was the first to respond.

Six

My mother couldn't control the weather in Seattle, but she could predict it. She picked one of the last sunny Sunday afternoons to keep us in a dim, hundred-year-old church for Christmas montage tryouts. The only hope streamed in through the enormous stained-glass windows, painting shards of colored light across the pews.

Mom wore her hair in a ponytail with a pen tucked behind her ear, looking like the hip director in a white tee and Editor pants. Everything was drawn on, from her eyebrows and plum-colored eyes to her mouth, as if a perfect exterior could mask a woman capable of spawning one hellion after another.

Everybody showed up to read for various parts, but Mom

already had her people staked out. Mrs. Hayes, the Kindly Old Woman (sorry, Mrs. Vandermar). Mr. Arthur would play the wise father. And I would be good old Brenda, the female lead. Which made it kind of sad that Essence showed up with "I wanna be Brenda" written all over her face. Even sadder, she deserved it.

Essence's bedroom had always been lined with show posters where she had played a chorus bird or a maid or, more recently, the lead's best friend or mother. Delaney was right. She wasn't lead material. She was chunky, whiny, on the underside of pretty. Just right for comic relief. *Someone who's holding you back,* Delaney had said.

Essence stayed after church to help set up for auditions, and I realized I was part of this bizarre love triangle: Essence wanting my mother's attention and my mother wanting mine. If only Essence was my mother's daughter, then everybody might be happy.

"How was your summer?" I asked.

"Fine."

We were in the same spot where we'd met in second grade, the day Xanda showed up at the Mother's Day fashion show in a dress identical to mine and Mom's, only hers was shredded and paired with biker boots. We landed on the front page of the *Seattle Times'* "Arts and Living" section under the headline PRETEEN PUNK FASHIONISTA CRASHES CHURCH FUNDRAISER—the succubus, the church lady, and me. A new girl stood by in awe—about my age, with freckles and a tan from someplace far removed from the Northwest. She and her mom wore long, crinkled skirts and peasant blouses with strands of clay beads. Definitely not from Seattle.

The girl came up to me after the show, bubbling over with smiles and excitement. "That was your sister?" I nodded. I could hardly believe it myself.

Before long, we were inseparable, even if my sister found her annoying and my mom found her undesirable—Essence's family fell in easily with Seattleites militant about fair trade, growing their own organic food, and recycling everything from plastics to clothing—exactly what my mom found distasteful about the Northwest. When her mom joined the prayer chain, mine made sure she was on the opposite end. Still, Essence tried out for every one of my mom's plays without fail.

Apparently some things hadn't changed.

"Honey," my mom called from upstage, "could you read some of this script? I'm trying to see if it will be a good section for the tryouts." Which was weird, because clearly she had already put painstaking thought into every detail. My reading would be of no consequence.

Essence jumped to my mother's side. "I could read, Mrs. Mathison," she gushed. "I think your work is amazing. In fact—"

My mom barely gave her a glance. "All right, Essence. How about you read for the father."

"The father?" Essence's smile faltered. "Um, okay, Mrs.

Mathison. But I'd really like to try out for the part of—"

"Mandy, you read for the part of Brenda." Essence looked like she wanted to take my mother right up to the baptismal waters and introduce her to some redemption. But she took the script.

The two of us got up on the stage, towering over the pews. I tried not to think about performance night, when they would be filled and each line I spoke would be a nail pounding into my throat. I never wanted to be on this stage again.

So the two of us read while my mother blocked out the scene with masking tape. Essence made a better father than I made a Brenda. I would have told her if she hadn't been giving me the nastiest look she could muster—prim, exaggerated, almost cartoonish. At that moment I could see her exactly the way Delaney did. Part of me hated myself for it.

When others started showing up, my mother waved us down. "Don't want to let any cats out of the bag," she sang. If any cats were going to escape, I was hoping to be the first.

"All right," Mom said in a loud, competent voice, "I want to keep this fairly simple. We'll do leads first, then the supporting cast so I can get an idea of whose talent is suited for what." This was the control-freak dream—everyone looking to her to tell them what to do. Everyone but me. She started handing out a stack of script excerpts, and then dumped the remainder in my lap. "Mandy, help me out here."

As I passed out the scripts, I couldn't help but glance over the paragraphs she had typed up for the tryouts: Brenda discusses faith with her father and newly cancered mother as they prepare to face the future together.

Barf. Her completely transparent vision for our family. Even worse, Brenda was probably some weird fusion of Xanda and me: the prodigal girl coming home.

When I finished handing out the scripts, I parked myself in the back of the room with my sketchbook while my mother directed three of the readers. Essence and her hissy *s*'s kept floating into my ears as she paced back and forth, reciting the lines in a stage mumble. Her voice reached that pitch that never used to bother me until Delaney pointed it out.

The stained glass, lit by the late-afternoon sun, found its way into my sketchbook. My lines tried to trace the shape of Jesus in the stained glass—*focus on faces*, my art teacher would say—but the pieces kept fragmenting and recombining into a spidery lair.

A blue patch of light stretched across my sketch and I smiled, remembering how Xanda and I used to draw pictures of the minister and choir. We would sit with Essence as far back from the minister as we could get away with.

Even at twelve my drawings were smooth, balanced, carefully rendered. Xanda's were angular and dramatic, with dark lines and unexpected details. Like the eyes of the soloist, one of them bigger than the other, or the too-loose blouse on the Elder after her mastectomy. Essence drew them as stick figures, acting out their secret sins on a stage and sending Xanda and me into snorts of laughter.

One Sunday Xanda and I sat in the very back pew while the minister preached on the deadliest of the deadlies: pride, vanity, and envy.

"Let's draw them," Xanda whispered to me. I thought of what pride would look like, a jowly old guy in a smoking jacket. Vanity was a tall, beautiful woman with a face like a mask. Envy was a treasure-hoarding dragon, dainty and diabolical. As I sketched in the dragon's face, I gave her eyebrows like mine, my turtle necklace around its scaly neck.

Xanda drew them as cliffs and valleys, irrevocably linked—pride as a mountain, envy a valley, hating its lowness and longing to reach, overtake, conquer. She drew vanity as a volcano with an abyss at its core.

Xanda took my drawings and eyed them critically. Hers said everything I wanted to say, the giddiness of pride and the void of envy. I waited for her to shred mine, tell me how they didn't measure up. The sticky pout of her mouth could go either way—dazzling smile or frown or even a spontaneous combustion.

A giggle erupted, causing one sour lady to purse her lips with a gigantic "Shhhh."

Xanda's hand flew to her mouth. "Did you realize this dragon looks like Mom?"

I could see it—the brows we shared, the heavy-lidded eyes. The dragon was not me, it was Mom.

"And Mr. Pride here looks like her, too," she whisper-laughed. We giggled together at the paradox of our mother, both pride and envy, the mountain and the valley.

"Well, I think that's a wrap," my mom said now as she approached me. Everyone else was already chatting in groups, with Essence scooping up empty latte cups and leftover scripts. Her thoughts were written on her face: Maybe this time she would get the part.

Mom peered over my shoulder onto my sketchbook, eyeing my drawing of spiderwebbed Jesus. I had given him stained-glass scales and a sweeping tail.

"I'll never understand the way you see things, Mandy," she sighed. "You take a beautiful drawing and turn it into something hideous."

"It's just a drawing, Mom," I replied, closing the sketchbook. "So how did the tryouts go?"

"Well, let's say I saw what I needed to see." She smiled and patted me on the shoulder. "I'll be posting the results next Sunday. This is going to be fabulous!"

A flash of Brenda the Bad popped into my head: hair tightly bound, holding her belly, monologuing about redemption. Not the Brenda my mother had in mind.

On the way out of the sanctuary, I snapped a phone pic of stained-glass Jesus. I would finish my drawing later.

Seven

"Miranda, what's the holdup?"

The next weekend, Delaney and Chloe were in my room getting ready for Milo's first party of the year. One more tour through my closet didn't produce anything but a paint-splattered T-shirt and a couple of skirts I knew would be too tight.

"Whatever possessed you to wear that?" Delaney asked me, giving my yoga pants and tee a withering look. I wondered if Delaney would be able to see right through me the way Xanda always could.

I shrugged. I didn't tell her my regular clothes had started to hurt, and the pressure made me want to hurl. Hoodies and fat jeans were my new uniform.

"Oh, whatever," Delaney said. "I know you've got some great stuff—"

"—that has somehow made it into your closet," I countered. Chloe snickered and held up an abandoned slip dress.

Delaney dropped her mascara into her purse and rolled her eyes. "Stand aside."

While she rummaged in my closet, I dove back into the bowl of cheese puffs. I couldn't get enough of them these days, now that my nausea had mostly morphed into a relentless, terrifying hunger.

"Don't you have a red bra someplace? I could swear . . . aha! Here it is." A wide-necked red top and bra flew out, landing in a heap.

"Wait. A. Second. Oh, my God!" Then came the sound of a million pennies sliding into each other. The veins in my throat closed. "You have to let me wear this!"

I knew what she'd found even before she emerged from the depths, the tinkling of metal on metal as clear as the day I'd first put it on. Chloe sat up with interest.

"This is magnificent!" Delaney held the safety-pin dress in triumph as she emerged from the closet. "Where did you find this? Did you *make* it?"

"Put it back."

"Oh, please, you can't just hide this—"

"Put it back!" As soon as the words escaped, I wanted to suck them back in. Chloe looked shocked.

"Of course. *The sister*. I should have guessed." Delaney

handed me the dress, letting the chains slip through her fingers. "Though you should wear it sometime. It would look amazing."

We finally came up with outfits—me in a plaid skirt and shiny boots, a Lolita for the new millennium. Xanda would be proud—not that I could say it. Not after Delaney stopped me in front of everyone last spring and said, "You keep talking about your dead sister. It's creeping me out."

As I looked in the mirror, I admired my new body benefits. Chest, even hips. More and more, I saw my sister. My waist, on the other hand, seemed to be a thing of the past. Any day now, Delaney would gently suggest I lay off the puffs.

I wanted to tell them. I was dying to tell them. Chloe might be a shoulder to cry on, and Delaney—Delaney would know what to do. "Wait, I have something to tell you." Chloe looked at me with her round brown eyes, and Delaney looked up before carefully applying another layer of eyeliner. "What?"

But saying the words would make it too real. I wasn't ready for that yet. Instead, I pointed to my clock. "It's nine already. We'd better go!"

At the end of a long road of dilapidated dwellings sat the shack Milo shared with his brother. The shack had been the site of many an Elna Mead party. Delaney and I had been here plenty last spring—she and Milo became fast friends after she was kicked out of View Ridge Prep. Tyvek sheets served as curtains—bachelor decorating at its best. Even the walls and shaggy brown carpet were permeated with the odor of one

48

too many parties. My mother would be appalled.

Crammed inside the house was every person under eighteen I knew, bodies crushed like cigarettes and pulsing to the beat of a ginormous stereo. As I looked around the room, lit up by a red bulb in the corner, faces slowed down into grotesque laughter and shouts of greeting. Everyone was glad to see us—the leggy one, the curvy one, and the one who could stop Elna Mead traffic. I reached inside myself and pulled out "party girl," modeled after Delaney and Xanda herself. I smiled at the faces around me, calling out loudly and giggling. The real me floated up to the corner of the room.

"Hey, hey, hey, look who's here," called Milo, raising a frothing plastic cup in greeting and sloshing half of it onto the carpet. He spotted the bottles we carried. "Even better—keg's in the back."

"*Salut! Comment ça va?*" Delaney declared to a group smoking ultrathins and sipping cups of Two Buck Chuck. They had already commandeered a couch whose right side had long ago ceased keeping up with the left. "Here," she said to me, handing me the bottle of Sapphire. "Take this back for me?" Chloe handed hers over, too, and they both wove their way to the couch to *voulez-vous* with the French contingency.

The bartender's back was turned when I approached, mixing cheap vodka with orange juice. But I knew that form. I even remembered the white shirt I could never get her to wear because she thought it was too revealing. "Just chill, be there in a second." The voice crackled like Styrofoam.

How Essence ended up at this party, I didn't know—then again, she had found her way to Delaney's cabin last July. At least this time, Delaney wouldn't think I invited her.

I set the bottles down on the counter with a clunk. "Here." Essence spun, fresh drink in hand with a sprig of mint peeking out.

"No, thanks," I said. "Just juice."

"Oh, it's you. Get your own."

"Whatever," Delaney said behind me. The two of them bristled for a moment. Then Delaney laughed, as if Essence's defiance wasn't even worth registering. "Sorry," Essence mumbled, so that even her extra layer of chub seemed deflated. She poured me a glass of OJ.

You can't buy that kind of power. Essence, God help her, had dared to cross it.

"You've got to be kidding me," Delaney had laughed. It was last spring, after I'd been spending more and more time with Delaney and less and less with Essence. "She thinks I'd try to steal *Eli*? As in, *Autoerotic Eli*?"

I blushed, remembering I had come up with that brilliant moniker myself. "Well, you do flirt a lot, but Essence thinks . . ." I stopped, feeling annoyed. It was getting easier to blame Essence for a lot of things.

That was the day Delaney took me to her brother Dylan's house for the first time.

Delaney wound her car around traffic circles and hills

while everyone else was slaving over fifth period. She parked across from a house that looked like the last holdout in the war on weeds, badly in need of a paint job. The porch door hung open with a note stuffed into it saying, *BBL, needed Stuff—D.*

"Crap." Delaney shoved the doorknob. We spilled into the living room, a weird combination of IKEA and abandoned-on-the-sidewalk decorating. We sat down next to the picture window to watch for Dylan.

"Come on, Rand. I can't help it if Eli thinks I'm hot. It's not like I'm *doing* anything to get his attention—are you kidding? And I don't mean to be bitchy here, but if you're comparing me and Essence . . . well . . ."

"I know." I backpedaled. The insult to Essence didn't even really register. "You're right. It's just . . . this is her first boyfriend."

"I can't help that," Delaney said callously, switching from interest in the window to hunting through a hunk of her hair for split ends. "I don't know why you hang out with her anyway. All of her whining is rubbing off on you."

"We have a history," I said. I didn't tell her the whole truth—Essence was woven into our family like another sister, stripped away thread by thread since I had met Delaney.

She located an elusive split end and plucked the entire hair right out, as if its very imperfect existence was offensive to her. "People are starting to notice you, Rand. *Guys* are noticing you."

I blushed. "Really?" I thought of my sister, whose presence

commanded attention in ways I never could. The same way Delaney did.

Her smile was encouraging. "Yes, really! You hadn't noticed?"

"Well . . ." The truth was, I had. At parties, clubs, places that had once been closed to me—as long as I was still with Essence.

"Essence is exactly what you said—your history," she said gently. "Maybe it's time to leave history behind you and see what the future holds. Besides," she added lightly, "I'm tired of sharing you."

Essence and I weren't even really friends anymore. Different interests, different friends. She was embroiled with Eli and drifting further into the drama crowd, and I had Kamran on my horizon. She probably wouldn't even miss me, and if she did, we were still partners in chem lab, and I still saw her at church and in Mom's drama productions. The logic of it only magnified the swell of happiness I felt at being chosen by Delaney.

And though she hadn't come right out and said it, Delaney was giving me an ultimatum: her or me.

Delaney hopped up. "I'm sick of talking about Essence. Let's get a beer."

I followed her to the fridge, collaged with rent checks, naughty magnets, and tiny black-and-white fragments of poetry.

Then I saw it.

The photograph.

Xanda.

A picture of my sister, Andre, and a guy who had to be Delaney's brother, Dylan—mouths open in exaggerated laughter, piled haphazardly on the couch where I'd just been sitting. Xanda, who looked as alive in that photograph as the day she walked out our door. Heavy-lidded eyes like mine, the same age I was right now. It could have been me in that picture. And strangely, Andre could have been Kamran.

And suddenly the choice between Essence and Delaney became much simpler.

"I can't wait to bring you to one of Dylan's parties," Delaney was saying as she poked around in the fridge. "They're unreal. And my brother would think you're completely hot." She got a sly grin on her face. "But then, you've been hanging out with a hottie of your own these days. What's his name again?"

Eight

Milo's party got off the ground now that Delaney was here. She balanced the French group on one side and the skaters on the other while Chloe learned the finer points of beer chugging from Milo himself. Kamran had said he was going to stop by. I craned my neck looking for him and checked my cell phone for missed calls.

"Looking for Kamran?" Delaney shouted over the boom of the stereo. "He's not coming."

I felt a thud in my chest. "How do you know?"

"What?" she shouted.

"Why not?" I said, with more force.

"He called me a couple of hours ago—said he had to go in to work and wasn't going to make it." She shrugged. My disappointment must have registered on my face, because she gave me a quick air kiss and a grin. "It's okay, Rand! We'll live without him!" All I could do was gape at her smiling face. I tasted a trace of acid and knew what was coming next.

"Be right back," I mumbled.

"'Kay, honey." And she was yanked away while Milo held a shot aloft and ordered, "Here, your turn!" amid more laughter and shouting.

I had to push past the drama crowd, entrenched in one of the bedrooms, to get to the bathroom, a creepy little space with doors on either side and only a couple of rickety hooks to keep the crowd from crashing in. The smell, the close quarters, the idea of thousands of germs festering on the toilet seat, were too much for me. I hurled just as one of the hooks gave way and the door swung open. Essence was standing there, her eyes wide as beer mugs. "Oops," she blurted. She clamped her hand over her mouth, trying to hold back the hoots of laughter exploding out of her.

Everyone gathered to see what was so funny, and the real me—lurking at a safe distance—pounded back into my brain with a crack.

I heaved my way out of the bathroom right up to Essence, who was holding her sides with one hand and a huge cup of beer with the other. Her body bounced with laughter, the cup teetering in her hand. The shame drowned out any memory of our old friendship. I pushed past, giving her elbow a slosh, and the group scattered to avoid the cascading liquid.

The laughter shifted to Essence, beer penetrating her too-white, too-tight shirt and dripping down her legs.

"Oh my God, look at the cross-your-hearter on those mothers!" someone shouted, maybe Milo. "Hey, everybody, wet T-shirt contest in the bedroom! Saaa-weeet!"

The anger burning in my throat settled back down into a dull ache as Delaney burst on scene, followed by half the house. Essence's eyes locked with mine.

"Rand's had a little too much to drink," Delaney said, taking my hand and trying to steer me to the door. But she couldn't resist a giggle when she saw the fabric clinging to Essence's skin and the grandma pattern of her bra.

"She's had orange juice!" Essence shrieked, but no one was listening. It was a victory, though it felt more like I had slammed a door and locked it behind me.

Delaney dragged me outside with Chloe not far behind. The cool air couldn't chill me to the bone any more than Delaney's look. "What the hell happened?" she demanded. Chloe stopped giggling on the spot.

I held up my glass of orange juice, my feeble excuse. Her fists were on her hips, her head swinging back and forth.

"I know you weren't drinking anything, so what's going on?"

Chloe stared at me with a mixture of curiosity, admiration, and horror. Both of us were holding our breath, waiting to see what would happen.

If only Kamran were here. If only he had called me instead of Delaney.

I crumbled right there on the porch, which rattled with music and the wild laughter still echoing in the bedroom. Something drastic was in order. Tears sprang from nowhere, and I couldn't stop them.

Chloe put her arms around me and Delaney followed suit. Here, swallowed up in their friendship, I almost felt safe.

"I need you guys so much right now," I sobbed. "I'm so scared."

Delaney and Chloe held me tighter. "Just tell us what's the matter so we can help," said Delaney.

Chloe echoed, "We'll always be here for you." We sank down on the front steps together, ignoring the cigarette butts and bottle caps.

"I've taken two tests now." It felt exciting to say, because I hadn't even let myself feel the realness of it until the words tumbled out of my mouth. A bubble of happiness floated up, followed by a rush of tears. "I'm pregnant."

"Oh, God," Delaney said. "Have you told Kamran yet?"

I shook my head. "And you can't tell him!"

"What are you going to do?" Chloe asked. She was crying, too. Delaney, though, looked thoughtful. "I can go with you," she said.

"You mean to the doctor? I haven't even thought that far ahead."

"I mean to the clinic. You're going to get rid of it, aren't you?"

A million thoughts spun through my head at once. I

wanted to say yes. I wanted to scream no. I wanted to follow Delaney's lead and let her take care of everything. I wanted Kamran back. And a baby. His baby. Because without a baby, I knew where things were headed. *But with a baby?* There was really only one hope left.

"I don't know," I blurted out. "Maybe not. I mean, we're planning to be together, both of us going to school, and having a life together and everything . . . I guess maybe we'll just get married sooner." I ended lamely. *Married.* It came out of nowhere. But then, I felt a tiny triumph, seeing the look of shock on Delaney's face. Maybe they had a past together at Big Boss, but he and I had a future. Chloe gasped and put her hand over her mouth, shivering.

Thunk. A car door slammed on the side of the house, and all three of us jumped. Essence's car—a clunky yellow hatchback—rolled past on the gravel road, spitting rocks. Her eyes met mine through the window, and she smiled darkly.

My God. I hoped she hadn't heard.

Nine

Essence didn't come to school today, but her legend lived on. She was no longer Essence, but the far nobler creature, Cross Your Heart. Milo spread the gospel far and wide. "Cross Your Heart! It was fan-freakin'-awesome!" I heard people talking who hadn't even been there.

Which was good, because it meant nobody would be talking about me.

Delaney knew. Chloe knew. And then there was Essence.

She hadn't even looked in my direction at church. Mom didn't notice my puffy eyes—or the shapeless, drooping excuse for my Sunday best. She was too busy posting the results of the Christmas montage tryouts and the rehearsal schedule beginning in a few weeks. Dad didn't seem to notice me at all. He sat at the back of the sanctuary and snuck out early to work on his latest job. I kept my eyes on stained-glass Jesus, hoping he could find it in his heart to forgive me.

I kept calling Kamran, but he must have already gone to Big Boss. The line went straight to voicemail, the same greeting since always: "Kamran. Hey. Speak." Was Delaney still working there? He'd probably talked to her ten times by now, severely testing her vow of silence.

I didn't leave a message.

In English class on Monday, Kamran came in at the last minute and was the first to leave. Not once did we make eye contact. When I touched his arm as the bell rang, he jumped back like I'd slapped him. He said nothing, only threw his pack over his shoulder and disappeared around a corner.

Delaney swept me into the bathroom before my last class. She looked sparkling, her hair loose and framing her face. Last time I checked, I looked like I'd swallowed a dead cat. "I just saw Kamran. He seems pretty upset . . . ," she began.

The dread swirling around me all day settled into a giant lump in my chest. "You told him?"

"Of course not, but Essence . . . I think she heard us talking . . ."

I'd seen Essence with a few people from the drama crowd, surrounding her and looking as menacing as if they were the Jets and I was a Shark. I'd never seen her look that mean before. Would Essence have told him?

Delaney pulled lip gloss out of her bag and handed it to

me. "I could talk to him for you. We hung out a lot over the summer . . ."

My face must have given me away, because she stopped and took my hand. "Rand, I just want you to know, whatever happens, I'll be there." She looked so sincere when she said it, I suddenly felt an avalanche of guilt for every suspicion I'd ever had.

"Thanks," I said.

I had choices to make about this pregnancy, every one leading to something final. When to tell Kamran? Abort or keep? I knew I couldn't tell my parents. If Xanda couldn't help me, Delaney would be the next best thing.

AP art found us practicing medieval perspective—except for me. I was banned from doing anything remotely resembling labyrinths. "Try portraits," Mrs. Crooker had said. "It would be a good exercise for you. Loosen you up. Besides, you will need to show your breadth if you want to get into Baird."

My assignment was to draw the student next to me. After I blocked in the head shape, the features, the hands holding the pencil, I zeroed in on the paper beneath—spiraling through a medieval city, along corridors, down staircases, into my own private path to the spider's nest. When the teacher dropped by, she rolled her eyes in exasperation. I lingered after class, finishing the ever-shrinking path in my drawing. Maybe I could avoid the inevitable.

I had to tell him myself, before someone else did.

I found Kamran after the final bell rang—not at my locker, but at Delaney's. The two of them were cozied up like two old friends, laughing; not at all like they were feeling the weight of the future.

When she spotted me, Delaney's smile shifted from coy to the kind of smile she might give to someone dying—pity, mixed with a tinge of survivor guilt. Kamran's gaze followed me darkly.

"Hi, sweetie," Delaney cooed, putting her arm around me. "How are you feeling?"

I muttered, "Like crap."

"Come with me, I've got just the thing," she said, steering me toward the bathroom. "I got a new—"

"I don't want to come with you. I need to talk to Kamran." She looked surprised and a little hurt.

"Oh, okay. Do you—"

"Delaney, don't," Kamran snapped suddenly. "This isn't something you can fix."

Fix. Oh, God.

He grabbed his pack and stormed past me, leaving Delaney to scurry off with a "You guys have some stuff to work out, I guess. I've gotta find Chloe before she has a panic attack." As if I wasn't having one right here in front of her.

I followed Kamran out to his motorcycle, where he had already put on his helmet and revved the engine. A piece of tape covered the tear in the seat where I was always scratching my leg last spring. It curled upward, like a Band-Aid that just needed to be ripped off.

I straddled the front wheel. "Kamran," I shouted over the rumble. Who cared if people were staring. "Kamran, we have to talk!"

He tore the helmet from his head while the engine still growled.

"Yeah, you've been doing a lot of talking, it sounds like. Only not to me." I'd never heard him use this tone before. Usually he was totally unflappable. Now his voice rose to an alarming volume.

People were curious. They gathered, though not close enough to be a target for a hurtling helmet, should he decide to throw it. Students sitting in their cars discreetly rolled their windows down a crack.

"Kamran, I tried to call you. I've been trying to reach you all summer, and you didn't return half my calls."

"I was busy. I was working. And you call me a thousand times just to 'hear my voice,' so it's hard to know which calls are the important ones."

A few people snorted. Even teachers were watching now, stopped by their cars.

"I tried to call you yesterday," I said. "I tried all day, and you never called back."

"You called to inform me we were getting married? Like you told your friends and God knows who else Saturday night? When, exactly, is that supposed to happen? When I'm at MIT?"

A group of Hacky Sackers stopped Hackying, except for one disinterested dude who kicked the bag up and down with the cadence of a time bomb.

"Oh," he laughed, so that his jaw tilted up and I could see his neck constricting, "and here's the best part."

Oh, God, he already knew. *Please don't say it. Not here in front of everyone.*

"No," he said, "We're not going to go there. I'm not going to do this anymore. In fact, I was going to tell you this summer if it wasn't for the last time . . . forget it."

"Wait a second." I was still straddling the front wheel as he backed out. "Wait a second. Is this . . . Are you breaking up with me?" It was me, the skaters, the basketball players trickling out of the gym, waiting on the edge of a razor to hear his reply.

His eyes flashed sadness—and fear. "You lied to them," he said, his voice barely rising above the bike. "I can't believe you lied." He said the last part almost to himself.

"You didn't even tell me . . . it's like you did it on purpose." He broke off, for the first time seeming to notice we had an audience. "I'm sorry, I've got to get to work." He shoved his helmet back on his head and revved once more.

"But wait—you didn't give me a chance—" My words drowned as he sped off, and I was left to stand in the parking space alone. *I didn't even have a chance to tell you myself.*

No one else wanted to hear the news, either. As soon as he left, the lurkers dispersed.

"Dude, that was harsh," one of the Hacky Sackers said before kicking the bag across the circle.

Maybe my mom was right. Maybe I did take something beautiful and turn it into something ugly. Maybe what was supposed to be beautiful in another timeline had somehow turned rancid in this one.

I glanced at the double doors of the school's main entrance. Delaney stood there, watching.

Ten

When I came home, the house was eerily quiet. Usually I could count on Mom chatting to herself as she wrote, or on the phone with the prayer chain. Silence meant she was probably at the church getting ready for the first rehearsal. Which meant I could grieve my own private grief.

My stomach—ravenously empty about every half hour now—protested too much for me to consider life's complex and looming problems. In Maslow's Hierarchy of Needs, starvation came before sorrow.

I padded up the stairs to my room with a tuna sandwich, balancing my plate on one hand and my broken heart on the other.

Nothing I knew about Xanda prepared me for this. She left

no roadmap for rejection, no secret blog. No notes on dealing with decimation. I had tried to pour Kamran into myself, filling those tunnels of despair left over from Xanda with tendrils of hopefulness, the way being with Andre seemed to fill my sister with a kind of tempered steel. Now that Kamran had forcibly ripped them out, I was reeling from emptiness. Imminent total collapse.

Just before I bit into the sandwich, Mom stormed through my door—white face exploding with pink. I'd seen this face before.

"No tuna!" she shrieked, slapping the sandwich out of my hand and sending it splattering onto the front of my dresser.

Before I could recover, she spun on her heel and fled to her bedroom—an old script for Xanda, but a new one for me.

I could only hear faint, muffled crying on the other side of the door. Maybe my dad had finally had enough. Maybe someone on the prayer chain was dying of a tuna-inflicted coma. The tightness rose in my chest when I considered anything else.

Like the reel of a bad movie, I saw Essence slinking around the corner at the party and tearing off in her yellow hatchback. First Kamran, then my mom. *Oh, God. Let it be anything but that.*

"Mom," I said, my voice quavering. "Mom, are you okay?" For a moment I considered fleeing before I could find out, but the door opened, revealing her towering, trembling figure.

"I got a call from the prayer chain," she said in an even

voice, belying the loose hairs she flicked away with a fist.

The prayer chain. Essence. Whose mom could set the entire chain in motion before the news reached my mom.

"I thought we could trust you," my mom spat. "I should have known something like this would happen, sooner or later."

It's not like I hadn't heard these words before—they were just never directed at me. "What do you mean?"

"Everyone is praying for us, for our *family*. For you and your"—she glanced down contemptuously at my nearly flat belly—"your *condition*." The words looked like poison in her mouth. "Everyone is talking about it."

Of course they were. Divine humiliation. I could think of nothing worse.

"Who is the father?" she demanded.

"What do you mean, who is the father? It's Kamran!" My parents had barely crossed paths with Kamran, but they knew about him. They knew his name, knew I spent time with him, knew he was headed for MIT. "Why would you think it would be anybody else?"

"Well, I didn't know. If you're having sex, God knows who you're having it with."

She took my silence as confirmation.

"How many people are you having sex with, Miranda?"

I'm not even having sex, I thought miserably.

"I had hoped after everything your sister put us through, you would learn something. That's why we sent you away for the summer, because we thought . . . well, apparently, it was stupid for us to think we could keep you from screwing the first boy who looked at you."

She grabbed her forehead as though it were paining her to even look in my direction. "Right now you're as dead to me as your sister."

I don't even remember the gasp escaping, or running down the hall and out the door.

I ran until I couldn't run anymore, over the hill and down to Madison Park's playground and picnic tables, empty in the late September cold and covered with bird crap. The restaurant on the dock showed signs of opening, but I had left my money at home. She never even told me why I couldn't eat tuna.

My feet found the trail, joining the few joggers who braved the heavy, pre-rain air. Little did they know they were jogging past the worst day of my life.

I made my way around the trail for hours—or at least, it felt like hours—until the chill, darkness, and an insatiable desire for a piece of toast forced me home. Dad might even be there by now, although I knew it was useless to look for salvation from him.

Mom would have already related the gory details. At the Hanson job or the Travertoli job or the City of Seattle job, he would get a call. He would listen, and then say he needed to work a few more hours. There was no way he would take the blame this time. He didn't even know Kamran.

The house seemed deserted—every light off, except for a faint glow. Dad's truck was in the driveway. I guess that was good news. At least they would be talking. My delinquency might be enough to put them on the same floor.

I tiptoed in, hoping to reach my room undetected. Maybe some Easter candy lingered, some marshmallows from camp. A pasta necklace from second grade.

The glow came from the dining room, where I could hear forks clinking against china, glass tapping the cherrywood of the table. A voice—my dad's—murmured a low cadence.

I had barely seen my dad since I came home from camp, so I'd forgotten the musky smell surrounding him when he'd been on the job. The way the dust settled in his hair, the cracks of his hands, the weave of his shirt.

My mom's voice interrupted at an urgent pitch. I heard my name.

They weren't talking. They were praying.

My stomach reminded me of the looming threat of starvation. After a final *amen*, I made my way to the table where a plate of food had been set for me. Peas, chicken, rice. No toast. I bowed my head quickly for appearances, though my prayer was more of the *help me* variety.

"It's nice of you to join us, Mandy," Mom said. I braced myself for yelling—maybe, if this had been Xanda, there would have been. I glanced at my dad for some kind of support, but he was busy counting his peas.

"Mom—," I started to say, but she cut me off.

"The only thing to do is to put it up for adoption." I half expected her to suggest abortion—I'd thought of it myself. But not now that everyone knew. Sometimes it was hard to tell her true religion—the one where God was involved, or the one where everyone looked good.

"Adoption," I repeated, considering the idea for the first time. *But it's mine. The decision is mine.* She wanted everything hidden; my dad wanted nothing more than to avoid conflict. What did I want?

"And starting tomorrow, you're not going to have anything to do with that boy." *That boy.* Like Andre. Though not at all in the ways I'd hoped. "As of tomorrow, the only places you'll be are school, church, and home."

"But Mom, what about my application—" Six empty slots still stood in my portfolio. Without them, I might as well kiss Baird good-bye.

"You can do art at home. And for that matter, we're going to have to seriously reconsider whether you're even going to art school." I opened my mouth to protest, but I only seemed to be swallowing dust. "As for your friends, you aren't going anywhere. As for Kamran . . ."

She continued the diatribe of what I would and wouldn't be allowed to do. An image flashed through my mind of Xanda's suitcase, bursting at the seams, found in the trunk of Andre's Impala. The safety-pin dress spilled out like a chain-link fence.

My dad scarfed down his peas and rice until Mom was

silent. "I forgot to mention," he said quietly, "I need to go over some plans for tomorrow's job. I'll be in the basement if anyone needs me." He got up and brushed off the seat, just in case he had left any dust.

Eleven

After dinner there was nothing for me to do but hide in my room. I tried dialing Delaney's cell. She picked up on the fourth ring, right before I was about to hang up. The speaker caught the tail end of laughter, cut it off with a breathy, "Hello?"

I caught a snippet of a male voice, then everything but the white noise stopped, right there with my heartbeat. "Rand?"

I could hardly hold the phone. "Delaney," I said. "Is Kamran there with you?"

"Kamran? No, honey. Why would you think that? You must have heard the radio."

I knew what I heard, and it wasn't KEXP 90.3.

"What's up?" she continued.

I was silent.

"Hey, listen, Rand," she said cheerily. "I can't talk now, but can I call you when I get home?"

I moved my mouth, but no sound came out. If it did, it might bring the house down on me.

"Okay, Rand," she continued, "I'll call you when I get home. I saw you guys out there in the parking lot. Hope everything's okay."

Click.

Kamran's words still echoed in my head. *You called to inform me we were getting married? When, exactly, is that supposed to happen? When I'm at MIT?* But we had talked about it—the two of us moving to Boston, going to school, being together, having a life. When he wasn't focused on tests and applications. When I wasn't filling my portfolio. When I wasn't partying with Delaney and grasping at memories of my sister. When I imagined our future. Was I the only one?

I thought about calling Chloe—unwitting party to my secrets, grafted friend. Already she'd been emailing me angel wishes and personality tests without actually writing a word. She would probably unload her cutesy best friend–ness on me, tell me everything would be okay and that she would be there for me, too. As I lay there on my bed thinking about her and Delaney, I got more and more angry. For all I knew, she was in on it, watching Kamran and Delaney flirting all summer and never saying a word.

Then there was the person I'd always talked to, intertwined with my family for more than half our lives and now separated by a span of mixed emotions. No, I definitely couldn't call Essence.

I needed to talk to someone, and Xanda wasn't around to meet me at midnight, right after she had been out with Andre and smelling of dampness and leaves and French fries and skin. All I had was a safety-pin dress.

Mom retreated to the bedroom and anesthetized herself with her scripts. Maybe she'd change her Brenda character from the prodigal daughter to the prodigal *pregnant* daughter. I would look the part in a few months.

"What are you doing?" she demanded when I tried to slip into the office, as if Kamran lurked outside and we were going to have sex right there.

"Homework."

"You'd better be." And she went back to her steady drip of imaginary characters.

The internet window popped open and I plugged in my search. The results for "teen pregnant dumped completely screwed" didn't look promising. On the BabyCenter website, the question of the day cheerfully asked, "My pregnancy test showed positive. Am I pregnant, or could it be something else?"

I plugged the date of my last period into the little due date calculator, though I couldn't even really remember anymore. Right when school got out. The week after, maybe. Definitely before the cabin trip. If my guess was right, I was fifteen weeks—almost four months—pregnant. Fifteen out of forty.

I reached for the snack I'd raided from the kitchen, some crackers and an apple. I followed the thread, where people gave advice, suggested courses of action, and offered varying levels of medical-babble. The "community" section promised boards for every possible fertility contingency. I couldn't help it—I was sucked in.

I clicked through some links to the list of bulletin boards—advice for dads, grief and loss, first-time pregnancy, teen pregnancy. Foods to avoid, like tuna. I wondered how my mom knew. Questions like, "My chest hurts. Is this normal?" populated the board in a limitless spiral of subjects under discussion. There didn't seem to be one for my situation: how could I go back to before everything began?

The Teen Pregnancy section was mostly filled with fourteen-year-olds panicking about what to do when their parents found out. I already had enough panic in my life.

But there was something appealing about the First-Time Moms section. They were newlyweds, or trying for so long they'd almost given up, or surprised by babies completely disrupting their lives. What they had in common, though, wasn't fear or resentment. More like joy. They had handles like "babyfairy" and "soon2Bmom" and "stacy+one." They wrote about morning sickness and tests and ultrasounds and their spouses, putting in smiley faces and baby meters to show their growth. Babyfairy was the fantasy-philiac. Soon2Bmom was the executive. FemmeNikita stood out as the leader, or at least the most outspoken, who wrote stuff like, "This is the most fun I've had since sperm met egg."

After an hour reading through their posts, they felt like friends. They made pregnancy seem like fun, even freedom. Out in the ether, I could make things the way I wanted them to be. The way I hoped they still could.

I didn't sign up, but I had already thought of the perfect screen name:

XandasAngel.

Twelve

Delaney didn't call me back. Suddenly she had a million errands to run and couldn't look me in the eye, except to stop after our History class and say, "I heard about you and Kamran. We'll have a chocolate night soon, okay? Gotta run now—French is kicking my ass this year. À bientôt!" Chloe's communiqués were limited to cute quotes and warnings to add an ICE—in case of emergency—number to my cell phone. Not that I had any idea who that might be.

I didn't have to worry anymore about everyone finding out, because now they knew. Between my parking-lot fight with Kamran, my so-called friends, and Essence's big mouth, the information spread like a virus. Instead of "Did you see Cross Your Heart today?" it was, "Did you see that wicked fight?" and "I heard she got pregnant on purpose."

Kamran could avoid me everywhere but English—we existed in separate, parallel universes. But his anger was palpable, impenetrable. I had to wonder if I'd seen the fear at all.

At lunch I headed to the library or computer lab, reading up on the halcyon pregnancies of FemmeNikita—aka Nik—and her peers. In that world, Kamran still loved me. Keeping the baby meant keeping hope.

Things at home might have seemed normal if I were Xanda—the dark looks, the disapproval.

I should have known the second I saw the sleek, black car in the driveway that something was very, very wrong.

Mom rose to her feet when I entered the house, and so did a strange woman, coiffed and stiff as our living-room cushions. Brenda the Good would stay and greet the visitor, maybe even offer her some ladyfingers. Before my fall from grace, I would have done that, too. Now, what was the point?

"Mandy, I'd like you to meet—"

"—Miz Wrent," the woman cut in as she held out a hand shiny with moisturizer. My mom took a sip of tea. The two of them seemed to have formed an uneasy alliance.

Miz Wrent spoke. "Your mother has been telling me all about you, Mandy."

"Rand," I said. I felt my body start to slide into a state of panic—imminent hypoglycemia. In case of emergency, carry snacks. Even better: Pack a suitcase.

"Can I get you something to eat?" I asked, hoping my

politeness veiled my desperation. "A cookie or a sandwich?" She declined. My body growled in protest.

"No, I'm here to ask you a few questions before we start the pro—"

My mom cut in. "Miz Wrent is here from Social Services. She wants to help you make some decisions." Miz Wrent looked like there was a lot more she'd like to say, but instead she turned to me with a waxy smile.

"Are you sure I can't get you a snack?"

"No, no," she began, then suddenly the light bulb turned on. "Oh, but you must be starving. Get yourself something before we get started."

As I slapped together a sandwich, the two of them whispered. I strained to hear.

"Ms. Mathison—"

"Call me Hillary."

"Hillary. Does she know who the father is?"

"Yes."

"And will he want to be involved in this process?"

"Not if we can help it," my mother snorted. *He will if I can,* I said to myself as I dumped a glob of raspberry jam in the center of the peanut-buttered bread.

Miz Wrent's voice shifted. "It's a shame, seeing what a lovely home you could—" Then she stopped herself. Shifted back. When she spoke again, it was all business. "Has she been having any problems so far?"

"Oh, no," my mom responded, as if she even knew. "If

only we could all weather pregnancy as easily as a teenager. Do you have children?" I didn't catch the response, but they laughed conspiratorially. I wished I could wring my mom's stupid, haughty neck.

"What is her due date?" asked Miz Wrent as she recovered from the shared joke.

Yeah, Mom, tell her about the date. I didn't want to miss this opportunity to see her squirm. But Mom evaded—damage control was her specialty. "Mandy, tell Miz Wrent about your pregnancy."

"I'm not exactly sure." I made a show of counting. "Beginning of summer . . . nine months, right? June . . . July . . . this spring, maybe?" Who said I wasn't an actress?

Miz Wrent shored herself up. "Not exactly sure? Hasn't your doctor given you a due date?"

"I haven't been to a doctor," I said innocently.

"You haven't been to a doctor yet?" she demanded, giving my mom the "what kind of mother are you?" look. I couldn't help but feel a little smug.

"We haven't found the right doctor yet," my mom said, convincingly enough for a Tony. Behind the triumph, though, was a note of panic. Miz Wrent looked doubtful.

I smiled shyly. "Maybe you have a recommendation?"

"Of course. I'll leave you some information when I give you the paperwork I'd like you to fill out. Now." She gave my mom an unsure look. "I need to ask Rand some questions. Do you have any medical conditions—STDs, high blood pressure, diabetes—that could complicate delivery or endanger the health of the baby?"

"No, I've never—"

"Have you taken any drugs or alcohol since becoming pregnant?"

"No!"

My mother leaned forward, gobbling up my words as soon as they left my mouth.

"Would you be interested in meeting the parents in an open relationship, or would you prefer your information to be classified?"

I was turning a dangerous corner, about to step into a covered pit. "Why are you asking me all of this? What do you mean, meet the parents?"

The pieces slammed into my head like a puzzle of broken glass. *The only thing to do is put it up for adoption.*

I couldn't believe my mother had done this. I hated her. I wished I could kill her. And more than anything, I wished for Xanda's help. She had left me to grope in the darkness by myself.

Miz Wrent's relentless gears ground to a halt. "Excuse me, Ms. Mathison. You led me to believe your daughter wanted to give this baby up for adoption."

Adoption. I could see the path stretched out before me. I couldn't turn back now that they knew. There would be no art, no escape if I crossed this threshold and took what they offered. My parents would tighten the chains until I could no longer breathe. Like they did to Xanda. The only escape would be death.

If I said no? I could pack that suitcase and plan that escape and maybe, just maybe, Kamran would come. If I said no, there was still a chance for everything to change.

"I'm keeping it!" I shouted, upsetting the teacups. "You can't force me to give it up. I won't!"

Miz Wrent never did leave a doctor recommendation.

Thirteen

Before she spent her days and nights with Andre, Xanda and I would climb out the bathroom window to the side roof under Mom and Dad's bedroom window. Xanda would smoke while I drank one of Mom's contraband diet sodas. She dangled her feet over the edge, flicking her ashes into the garden below. I sat as close to the house as possible, always afraid of falling off. There we would listen to our parents' latest strategies for keeping Xanda in line.

Now I availed myself of the next best thing: hiding in the bathroom with the window cracked.

They were arguing. Or rather, Mom was yelling, and Dad was listening. Their voices were like jackhammers—my name, said over and over. *Mandy . . . Mandy . . . Mandy.*

They were arguing about me. More precisely, what to do with me. The options were limited.

"We could send her to stay with my parents," Dad was saying.

"Oh, no we won't," seethed my mother, as if he had suggested parading me around with a big red *A*. "You want her spending time with your sister? The one who can't keep a job and is still living with your parents in a *trailer*?" I knew the next part by heart: I didn't have to see Dad wince to know it happened.

"Well, if my parents aren't right, then how about yours? They could—"

"You can't be serious!" she countered. "I can't send a pregnant girl to go live with my family. . . ." She was as ashamed to send me to the white collars as she was to send me to the white trash.

"Fine," said Dad.

"There's only one thing to do. We'll stick it out, let her finish the school year, and then after it's all over, maybe we can move—"

Move? We didn't move because of Xanda, but they would move because of *me*?

"Hillary, we are not moving."

But Mom was not listening. "After this is all over, we could move back to Connecticut, or we could go to New Jersey . . ."

"Hillary."

". . . Nobody there would know, and then we could send her . . ."

"Hillary!"

Silence. Then: "What? You would let her ruin our lives here? Ruin everything we have worked for?"

You have worked for, I wanted him to say. The status, the money, the house on the hill. It was all about her, the rest of us be damned.

But he said nothing. A groan of disgust came from my mother. "I am not going to let you ruin everything again. *I won't.*" I thought she was finished. Then, in a much smaller voice, she said, "I've done everything different with Mandy. Where did I go wrong?"

Her words trailed away from the window, footsteps stomping into the hall before I could escape. I was trapped there in the dark, with only a night-light to guide me.

"Mandy?" The shrillness startled me. "Are you in there?"

What would Xanda do? I thought in a panic. Under other circumstances it might be funny, like I should have a WWXD bracelet on my wrist or tattooed around my ring finger.

I flushed.

Silence, for my mother, spoke volumes. It stretched out between us like hairs pulled from my head. She could control me with a few strands.

"Just going to the bathroom, Mom. Sorry I woke you up."

"Hmmmf," she said through the door. "Well, I'm going back to bed, then." Her feet shuffled away. The door of their bedroom shut.

As I crept down the hallway, their bedroom door sprang

open and my mom pounced.

"Your father and I have decided something." As if Dad had anything at all to do with it. "Since you have decided to *keep* this baby," she said with something clearly resembling revulsion, "you are going to stay in school until you have it. After that, we'll decide what to do."

"Um, okay," I said.

"But *don't be surprised* if we decide to move after the baby is born. In fact"—she looked down at my stomach—"you might think about starting to pack now." With that, she spun around and left me standing in the hallway with a slam.

She still had me caught by the hair, her hands straining to keep control.

What would Xanda do? That wasn't hard.

She would cut the hair off.

Fourteen

More and more, I spent my free time either in the art room or in the computer lab. Mrs. Crooker had pulled me aside after class one day and said, "Whatever happens, *you finish school.*" Even the lab tech must have heard by now, but he still only nodded sympathetically when I told him I was researching teen pregnancy for a class project. Which meant I could spend as much time as I wanted reading the BabyCenter boards.

According to the profile I submitted (code name XandasAngel), I lived in Seattle with my husband, was twenty-one years old and finishing my fine arts degree. Most of the other mommies had ultrasounds by now, and for all they knew, I was no different.

The morning after my parents' argument, I found a piece of paper slipped under my door in my dad's handwriting. "You'll probably need this to make a doctor's appointment. Love, Dad." The note was wrapped around an insurance card. The hormones raging through me now made it impossible to hold back tears. It would have been even better if he'd offered to go with me. The last thing I wanted was to go with Mom.

Hard to explain, but when I visited the board, all the stuff that sucked in my life seemed to go away. Kamran and I were happy together, Delaney was a loyal friend, I was following my dreams, and we were excited about the baby on the way.

When I posted, I introduced myself, my new life, and my most pressing pregnancy complaints: namely, weird cravings and the dreaded fat stage. Nik, "FemmeNikita," said, "Don't worry, honey, relief is only a few weeks away. You'll be doing the happy dance before you know it." I didn't see myself dancing any time soon. Besides, dancing made me think of Kamran and Delaney. I wished I could tell the other mommies about it, or at least Nik. For some reason I thought she would understand.

The tech was out and the lab closed, so I headed for the library to catch up with my new circle of friends. Nik was telling everyone about feeling the first kick, since none of the rest of us had experienced it.

Reading about Nik's baby made it even more obvious: I needed to tell the other moms the truth. I opened a new window and began to type the whole story—Xanda, Kamran,

Delaney. I was just about to send it when I heard a familiar giggle around the corner.

"That was a pretty harsh way for you to dump her," said the voice. Delaney. "I feel kind of sorry for her."

"I wasn't trying to be harsh." Kamran. I should have known he would be here, in between studying for the latest practice test, AP exams, and interviews. But I hadn't expected Delaney.

"You should have heard her, though, talking about you guys planning to get married right after school. I mean, for all you know, it's not even your baby. Did you actually *do it* with her?"

Kamran was silent.

"Oh, *no*, you *didn't*. Last summer? At my *cabin*?"

More silence. I could imagine him nodding gravely, maybe even with his head in his hands.

"But there were other guys, right? I mean, was she just trying to trap you? I would, if I had that family. Have you ever met them?"

Kamran spoke. "She's gotta deal with her stuff. I was always telling her."

Is that what he thought of everything I'd shared with him about Xanda? Stuff I had to deal with?

"I know, right?" Delaney agreed. "For the longest time all she talked about was her dead sister." One of them took a bite of something and the faint scent of pomegranates wafted through the bookshelves.

"She's been through a lot," Kamran said.

"Yeah, but she tried to drag the rest of us through it with her. I swear, she imitated me. I want a friend, not a doppel-ganger."

Outrage washed through me. Is that why she liked Chloe?

"I should have told her at the beginning of the summer. Stupid of me. I never should have let this get out of hand, and now . . ."

"You're not stupid. You're a nice guy. Nice guys do the right thing." Another giggle and the sound of a chair scoot-ing. "So . . . what do you think's in your future now, Mr. Nice Guy?"

I looked back at the long letter of truth I had typed to the BabyCenter girls, waiting for me to hit SEND. As long as I didn't, I could pretend none of this was happening—at least to them.

I logged off the computer and slipped out of the library without a sound.

I nearly collided with a few people from the drama crowd, though Essence wasn't with them. I put my head down and walked the other way.

It was fairly easy for me to avoid Essence these days—we hadn't planned our schedule together like we had every other year. But it was impossible to avoid her on Sundays.

Mom didn't say a word to me or Dad on the way to church. She hadn't said much since Miz Wrent's unceremonious departure. Instead, she spent every waking moment at her laptop—a new script, or maybe a memoir entitled *Humiliation: A Chronicle of Motherhood*. I had always wanted to be like Xanda, and now I was. I just didn't know it would involve this much guilt.

"So what have you been working on?" I asked my mom.

Dad glanced toward her for a split second. Mom continued to stare straight ahead, zooming toward the church at uncharacteristically high speeds. "I've made some changes to the Christmas montage."

I could see it already—if I wasn't sorry enough in real life, she'd make sure I would be onstage. No amount of repentance in real life would be enough. "What did you change?"

"You'll see." Then she turned her conversation toward my dad and the sets—how to construct the perfect alternate universe.

We arrived to a chorus of drama groupies whose whispers halted when we approached. I was stuck lugging in the box of new scripts. Mr. Warren (aka "Kindly Old Man") stepped in and said, "You shouldn't be carrying that." My mother didn't so much as bat an eyelash.

Essence was among the groupies. I was betting she couldn't wait for this moment.

If the rest of them were waiting around to witness the carnage, they obviously didn't know my mother. She took the stage with her usual, enviable composure. "All right," she said as she handed out the new scripts, "we've got some major changes in the works. I'm posting a new cast list as of today. Essence?"

"Yes, Mrs. Mathison?"

"You are taking over the part of Brenda."

Essence smiled. They deserved each other. "Absolutely. I already know Brenda's lines! I will *be* Brenda. Brenda and I will be one. So does that mean Miranda's taking my part?"

"No . . ."

Thank you, God.

". . . Claire will be taking over for you." Claire, a fourteen-year-old with perma-grin, squealed with happiness. "Mandy is going to be working on sets with her dad."

Essence snickered as she read over her script.

So that was it. I was demoted back down to set designer, a job I'd performed for half my life and even kind of liked.

Except for the first time since Xanda died, I'd had my own part in the play. For the first time, however briefly, the daughter my mom noticed was me.

Fifteen

After Miz Wrent's visit, I expected my mom to champion my health care, but all she said was, "If you're adult enough to get yourself into this, you're adult enough to handle the consequences."

It wasn't so difficult to see a doctor—just a quick web search and a phone call. I almost told Kamran in English class, where I watched the back of his neck the way I had a thousand times on the back of his motorcycle. But I couldn't. He gave me one look. Still angry. Scared. Maybe sad, too. Then he was gone.

When I arrived at the hospital, they gave me some paperwork and I handed them my insurance card. The nurse at the desk was horrified when she saw the date of my last period.

"June? And this is your first visit?" she asked.

"Yes."

"Oh, honey. I'll try to squeeze you in for an ultrasound today, too. We'll see how far along you really are." She handed me a water bottle. "Drink this."

The ob-gyn turned out to be this long-haired hippielike woman, only her sweater was pink with hearts embroidered on it. She had a kind face with bright blue eyes. After asking me a bunch of questions about my family medical history, she began asking questions about the pregnancy. I didn't know why, but I found myself pushing down the burning in my tear ducts. All of these things, from the moment I found out to the present, spilled out of my mouth and into the tiny hospital room.

She asked when I had my last period. Right at the end of junior year, though I couldn't remember the exact day.

I did remember the night the baby began, every detail. The way Kamran looked in the firelight. The way Delaney laughed and then paused to see who was watching her. Maybe we'd still be together, if that night had never happened.

Twenty of us went out to Delaney's dad's cabin for Fourth of July weekend: me, Kamran, Delaney, Milo, a few skaters, a few freshly graduated seniors, Chloe from French class, a few on the fringes of the popular crowd, and one unwelcome camper who somehow got the memo. That being Essence.

"Did you invite her?" Delaney growled.

"*No*, of course not. I have no idea how she found out." I knew it wasn't rational, but somehow it made sense to blame Essence. Because blame was so loud, it could drown out the softer, more insistent voice. *Shame.*

After taking the ferry across Puget Sound, Delaney led us up the path to her dad's waterfront cabin a mile or so from the docks. We reached the beach as the sun sank over the other side of the island. The boys grabbed some lighter fluid and sprayed the fire pit while I embraced the role of Delaney's partner in crime: "Milo and Ty, get some sticks from that grove over there." "Lin and Chloe, go get the booze." I felt powerful until I noticed Delaney standing off to the side, sharing a private joke with Kamran.

"Delaney!" She leaped to my side and smiled sheepishly. Once she was there, my mind went blank. *Stop flirting*, I wanted to say.

Kamran's face was unreadable. I knew what he would have said—they were just getting to know each other, the two best friends I'd always kept apart.

As we stoked the fire, Milo passed around a plastic cup of soda and something else to make us all feel a bit warmer in the cool, early summer air. After I had a few sips of Milo's concoction and the boys ran out of bottle rockets, I began to relax.

"What do we do now?" giggled Delaney after we'd made a circle around the bonfire. She tilted her head to one side and beamed—I thought—in Kamran's general direction. "There's always Spin the Bottle," she suggested coyly, "or Truth or Dare, or I Never, or—"

"I Never," I spoke up. Then I could have kicked myself. Was I that worried? I looked around the circle of faces, flickering golden in the firelight. They were laughing, drinking, talking, none of them paying much attention to me.

"I Never is good," Delaney said. "Everybody know how to play? Someone says 'I never . . . I dunno . . . screwed a purple dinosaur in the jungle.' If you have done it, you drink. Got it?" Murmurs of agreement followed.

The couples among us snuggled together. I knew after the game we would all stagger off to separate corners of the cabin, some of us with someone and some of us not. Kamran sat next to me, but we weren't touching. That was the way he liked it—no public displays of affection. He didn't want to make other people uncomfortable. "You know I love you," he would say. "Why do I have to prove it in front of everybody?"

"Who goes first?" someone asked.

Someone else said, "It was your idea, Delaney, why don't you go first."

Delaney sat to my left. That meant I would go last—plenty of time to formulate my statement. But I already knew exactly what I would say.

"I never . . . ," she drawled, smiling at the circle. I could see her eyes narrow as she located a target. "I never did it with Ty Belkin." Three girls sipped, each glaring at the other two. Ty stretched out his arms and grinned.

* * *

"We calculate the due date from the first day of your last period. That would put your due date around . . ." The ob-gyn paused. "March twenty-sixth, give or take a day. You're just beyond eighteen weeks now." March 26. Xanda's birthday. I thought it would be around the same time, but I didn't know it would be exactly that day. Again, I couldn't shake the feeling Xanda had something to do with this baby, that she had given me a secret gift. *XandasAngel*.

"Have you felt any movement yet?"

"No." I thought of Nik, telling all of us about her baby's flutter. "Is that normal?"

"You can start feeling it any time between sixteen and twenty-two weeks, but most first timers don't feel it until maybe twenty."

"What does it feel like?"

"Some women describe it as champagne bubbles," she told me. Then, giving me an appraising look, said, "Or soda-pop bubbles. Or, it can feel like a light tapping—like butterfly wings. The best time to feel it is at night, when babies are most active. Try lying on your back and waiting to see what happens. Would you like to hear the heartbeat now?"

I nodded. She helped me hop up on the table and pressed the end of a Doppler instrument into my flesh. It immediately emitted a static echo. Faintly, a deep, rhythmic thud emerged. I could feel my heart pounding, the sound echoing like a shadow. "Is that the baby?"

"No, that's you. I haven't found the baby yet." The knob rolled toward my hip, and the deep echo of my heart faded away. Another sound layered on top of it at a higher pitch—a smaller, faster *blip blip blip* underscored by the low, background thud.

"That's the baby. The heart sounds nice and strong."

"And fast!" I strained to commit the sound to memory. The digital screen read 150 beats per minute, now 156, now 148.

The ob-gyn smiled, adjusting the instrument. "Hello, baby!" she said to my stomach, and for the first time I realized it could hear me. "We can't wait to meet you."

The thought of it brought tears to my eyes. Happy tears, and tears of utter alarm.

Sixteen

After Ty Belkin's moment of truth, questions and answers blurred together until Delaney elbowed me merrily and said, "Hey, Rand, yooou've been dumped, haven't you? Drink!"

Huh? Was she talking about middle school? Did everyone else know something I didn't? Kamran raised an eyebrow.

Essence caught my eye from across the circle. An image of her ex–Siamese twin (Eli, attached at the tonsils) flashed before me: drama geek, smartier than thou, whose sole fashion statement consisted of badly fitted khakis and rugby shirts faded from washing out his pungent body odor. I couldn't believe Essence didn't notice. But I guess you could forgive a lot of things when you're the center of somebody's universe. As if Delaney would want to steal *him*.

As the game rippled around the circle and each person spoke their clever I Nevers, I stared at Essence, the contempt building in my throat. She didn't drink once, even though I knew she should.

The game stopped with her. She raised her head, eyes searing across the circle. For a moment, they flickered toward me with something else. Regret. Or sympathy. Then she looked straight at Delaney.

"I never tried to steal someone's boyfriend," she intoned, like a prophet of doom. The crowd burst out laughing, most of all Delaney. She looked stunning—hair caught up in two messy pigtails, gray eyes, movie-star cheekbones. She turned to me, inviting me to share in the joke, and for a moment I basked in the glow of her reassurance. Her gaze slipped past mine. I turned to see Kamran staring back, grinning. Then Delaney took a drink. A long drink. I had to get out of there. I had to pee.

Next stop: ultrasound, a room shrouded in warm darkness. I thought I was going to die, I had to go so badly—more and more the state of affairs these days, now that the baby was bigger. "Sorry, but we need a full bladder to see the baby," explained the ob-gyn.

The technician squirted some warm goo on my tummy and plopped the scanner right in the middle of it. She rolled it around, casting light and shadows into the connecting monitor. The white and black form mesmerized me, constantly morphing and completely foreign, like shadows and faces in a charcoal drawing. Finally a row of lines came into focus, a web of five long pips splaying into a recognizable shape.

"That's a hand," said the tech.

It was as though the hand unlocked the door. Suddenly I was able to make out an arm, then two arms. She showed me feet and legs, then back up to investigate a face emerging from the shadows.

"Do you want to know what you're having?" asked the tech.

"You can tell already?"

She laughed. "Do you have a sense of whether it's a boy or a girl?"

"No," I said, though I had a hope.

She rolled the scanner up to my belly button, and a U-shaped blob appeared on the screen. My heart slowed at the sight of the round shapes.

After Essence's I Never, I stumbled through the trees toward the cabin. Nettles snaked up and made itchy marks on my bare skin. My white shorts and tee, which looked so hot when I put them on, were now dusted with a layer of soot and the telltale imprint of my butt cheeks on the ground. So much for trying to keep Kamran's attention.

Well, what would Xanda do? For one thing, she would make the most of being dirty. She would be dirrrty. Grrr. "Grrr," I said aloud, then laughed at myself, as if Xanda were right there listening. "Okay," I panted, standing up straighter and putting my hand on my hip. "Let's try this again. Grrrrr!"

"Grrr, yourself," a low voice said out of the darkness. I could see Kamran's shape, lit up from behind by the moon through the forest canopy. His dark hair, grungy red tee, and worn jeans, just as dirty as mine and looking all the more delectable because of it, made me want to tattoo myself into his heart. We were alone. The campfire crowd hummed down the hill, laughter stretching out into blurry hoots.

So what if they were laughing at me, or if they weren't? Kamran had come.

"What happened back there?" he asked softly. Softly enough for me to wonder if I was imagining everything.

The choice spread out before me like threads in a labyrinth, here in this black forest. I could tell him the truth, my fears and insecurities laid out for him to dissect and dismiss. That road was well-traveled, and I knew exactly where it would lead. He could deny it all he liked, but I could see it clearly, even in the firelight.

Worse, he could confirm my fear—that in one moment, she'd captured his heart and stolen him away.

Or I could take another path, traveled by others but undiscovered by us. Delaney would have done it long ago, and she would have him wrapped around her finger. Here, with him looking at me like that, my "Grrr" still echoing in the moist heat and making me feel dirrrty and sexy and maybe even confident. Here we could discover a new path, past this present uncertainty and into a certain future. I could do that. I could take the chance. I could be more like Delaney in order to be more like me. In order not to lose him, I could take the first step.

A Roman candle went off in the distance. I took a step toward him, drawing his hands onto my hips where the skin touched my shorts.

I put my lips to his lips and sealed our trajectory: the undiscovered it was.

"Well, it looks like you're having a girl," the tech said, peering into the white shadows.

"A girl? How can you tell?"

She pointed to the screen. "Here is the bottom, where the legs come up, and then the three little lines in the middle. The three lines indicate girl parts."

I was in shock. "What would it look like if it was a boy?"

"A couple of big, round blobs," she laughed. "I don't know how people can mistake it."

I asked her to check again, just to be sure. But I knew already. I knew it all along.

"Do you have a name picked out yet?" asked the tech.

"Yes. Her name is Alexandra. But I'm going to call her Lexi."

Seventeen

Mom usually puttered around in the morning with Dad already gone, escaping the knot of our family tie. I came down starving, famished from an entire nine hours of producing another being. Even a fresh wave of condemnation wasn't enough to keep me from breakfast.

But the house was already empty. At least it seemed to be, when I came into the kitchen for my new obsession: grapefruit with oatmeal. *Meat for boys, fruit for girls*, the old wives' tales said. The BabyCenter women divided into two camps: those who were finding out and those who wanted a surprise.

When I posted Lexi's picture on the boards, Nik said, "You think you and Kamran are happy now, wait until that baby comes."

That's when she told us about her miscarriage. It was a year ago September. "She was my baby girl," Nik told us, even though it was too early to tell, only twelve weeks. "Her name would have been Lashaya."

Now that I had seen Lexi, I couldn't imagine what it would be like to lose her. Xanda was a preemie, but no one in my family had ever had a miscarriage that I knew of. I *did* know that if happiness was still possible, it would be because of her.

"What would you do if you lost Micah James?" I asked Nik.

"Faith manages" was all she would say.

A thud came from behind the basement door, and seconds later my dad came up into the kitchen. He looked as surprised to see me as I was to see him.

"Oh, Rand. Sorry, I didn't realize you were still here." He held a toolbox awkwardly, as if trying to hide behind it.

I held up the oatmeal canister. "How come you're still here?"

Dad shrugged. "Half the crew called in sick, we're behind schedule on the Cumberland project . . ." He ran a hand through his hair, releasing particles into the air as if we were bathed in spotlights. "Hey," he said. "Why don't I make us some pancakes?"

Pancakes were Xanda's favorite. As he mixed the batter and I got out the griddle, memories surrounded me—of how Dad used to make a big breakfast every Saturday with Mom and Xanda and me. Before he brought Andre into our lives and changed everything.

"So," he said as I carefully poured a syrup path through my pancake. "I'm starting to think about a design for the montage set. Your mom said you'd be painting this year."

"Yeah." He took a huge bite and waited for me to say more. He'd spread the batter thin, the way Xanda liked them. I wondered if he was trying to communicate in some special language for the grieving and forgotten. I wanted to ask him about Xanda, about Andre. I wanted to tell him about the girl. Lexi. Now was my chance to pour out my heart.

A shrill ring shattered the silence—his cell phone, with a call from his crew, the Cumberlands, Mom, it didn't matter. He stepped out of the room to answer while I scarfed down the rest of the pancake and folded up a second one to take with me. I had to get to school.

These days I avoided Kamran at all costs, even though I couldn't avoid him in English. I had no hope of focusing on the racial implications in *To Kill a Mockingbird* or illusions and reality in *Hamlet* with the back of his head in front of me. From that vantage, it was impossible to tell what he might be thinking—only that he darted out of the room the moment the bell rang, leaving the scent of figs and terror in his wake. Sooner or later, we would have to talk.

While I worked in the art room during lunch, my crazy art teacher stopped in now and then to check on my Baird application—due December 1, a little over a month away.

I had everything ready except for my final six slides, four of them freestyle pieces meant to reflect my personal aesthetic, the theme I would pursue if accepted into their art program. It wouldn't take a critic to see that every piece explored the same question: Could I retrace the turns of my sister's life and get to the very heart? Now there was a new question: Was keeping Lexi a terrible mistake?

And then there were the portraits. "You need at least two in there," Mrs. Crooker harped. "What is it about faces that sends you spiraling into those labyrinths?" I didn't tell her there would be only one person to draw. And that was impossible. Her face was always changing in my mind. The only photograph I knew of her was on Dylan's refrigerator—my mom must have destroyed all the rest.

The piece I worked on now was a charcoal drawing, since I'd been banned from toxic-fumed paint. I was starting to like charcoal, the graininess of it and the stark contrasts, for its similarity to the picture I now had of Lexi. The darks and lights emerged as I sketched lines, weaving in and out less like the sharp angles of my previous work and more like the curves and knots of how I imagined wormholes would be. Trails through time and space. Ways to capture the past.

"It doesn't work like that," Kamran had said when he first explained hyperspace to me, when I barely knew him. We had just spent three hours in the Sci-Fi Museum, where admiring Captain Kirk's chair and Robert Heinlein's original manuscripts was like sharing a religious experience. I could see exactly why my art spoke to him.

"You can't relive the past, because time is always splitting out from events—like infinite branches of a tree. Whatever choices you make affect the future."

I nodded my head like I understood, but he already knew me too well. Maybe that was one reason why I liked him—my masks didn't work. He only wanted the real thing.

"Okay, fine," I said. "If time is like a tree branch, why can't you go back to a specific point and change things?" I hadn't yet told him about Xanda. "Wouldn't it be possible, I mean, if you found the precise moment time shifted, the exact moment? Like the butterfly—"

"Right, right, like the butterfly and the tsunami—and if you could only trace back to the butterfly, you could—"

"Exactly!"

"No. You can't." His words stopped me, bumping into the fears I'd had since the beginning. He would think I was stupid. Unworthy. One day he would trade me in for a better model—someone more exciting, more clever. Like Delaney. "You can't do that," he was saying, "because it's impossible to go back to the same moment. You can't delete the time in between. It's like a branch trying to grow back into itself."

"Like a loop," I said.

"Yes! So I guess, *theoretically,* you could go to the same moment in time and space, but you would have experienced all of the time in between."

I could live with that—going back to the moment everything changed for Xanda, the point in time that would send her crashing to her death. I could trace back through the shards of memories, each scratching the surface of Xanda until she walked out the door forever.

"Nice," Mrs. Crooker commented over my shoulder. "Trying to break out of the labyrinth, I see."

As I worked with the charcoal, smudging it into a shadow of sky, a white shape had emerged—a bird taking flight. I abandoned the lines and focused on the bird, shaping it into a creature flying free, like the day Xanda tried to fly with Andre. Like I still hoped to with Kamran.

Maybe he was wrong. Maybe it was possible to change the present, if only I could pinpoint the exact moment everything had spun out of control.

That night, I sketched a picture of Xanda—what she might look like now, if she had lived to her twenty-second birthday. It didn't take long to start drawing labyrinths again. The curls of her hair spread out like Medusa's snakes—into her forehead, winding all the way into her mind and places I couldn't follow.

Unless all of this was some cosmic accident, I knew what that bird meant.

Somehow, through time and space and maybe even death, Xanda had reached across and offered me an escape.

Eighteen

The last weeks of October found everyone at school humming with party plans. Most of the jocks would be at Meghan McCaullay's house, sacrificing their brain cells to the great beer god and playing mix-'n'-match macking. The Goths would try to sneak into the Capitol Hill club Chains for a night of clove smoking and cauldronlike cocktails. There would be smaller parties, and parties too minor to make the radar, where people like Essence and the drama crowd would spend the evening bobbing for apples and wishing they had been invited to something better.

And then there was Dylan's bash.

"We *have* to go to Dylan's Halloween party next year," Delaney had told me last spring. "It's an Elna Mead legend.

He's been throwing them since, like, *his* junior year. You have to know him or one of his housemates to get in—but you'll be with me."

When I asked her about the party before class, she shrugged her shoulders. "I don't think he's having one this year—I was thinking about going to visit my mom in L.A. What are you doing?"

Apparently Milo didn't get the top secret memo, because now he stood in the hall with a stack of party flyers, handing them out with a lazy smile to any reasonably attractive female. "Heeeey, see you there?"

A pack of sophomore girls took the flyer, not realizing they had received one of the school's most coveted invitations. They giggled, rolling their eyes as they bustled by and let the paper flutter to the ground. I snatched it up, slipping it into one of my folders, completely unnoticed. It was like I no longer existed.

Or worse, too much of me existed, trying to negotiate the halls looking anything but sexy in my stretchiest jeans, worn low around my hips and under the small bump that had emerged, and a long tee getting shorter by the day.

I deliberately avoided looking at myself in the mirror, afraid of the unstoppable new me. Even my face, once taut and oval, puffed with what Nik had politely termed "water weight gain."

"It started out under my chin and took over," she complained on the chat board. "Water weight doesn't capture it—I think I'm carrying around a spare hot water heater."

It made me feel better to chat with the girls, hearing all of their pregnancy complaints. My stories were becoming increasingly outrageous as I tried to give the impression of a married college student. Kamran rubbed my back when it ached and went on cherry-chunk ice cream runs whenever I needed it. My parents were thrilled about the pregnancy and had offered to watch the baby while I finished school. I told them I was at the University of Washington instead of Baird, since the last thing I needed was to get caught by someone who actually lived there. Nik lived in the Northwest, too, and gave me her cell number, but I didn't call. I could imagine what she would sound like, though. Funny, matter-of-fact, never scared to tell the truth. Maybe she wouldn't hate me because I was.

"What are you doing for Halloween?" was the Question of the Day when I logged on.

Stacy+one was going to a party as a Mummy-to-be. Soon2Bmom and her husband would be Homer and Marge— only she would be Homer, compete with doughnuts and Duff while her husband teetered around in a green dress and blue wig. Babyfairy was sewing a knocked-up Maid Marian costume to go with her husband's Robin Hood, and Starr69 was hosting a party at her place and dressing up as Earth Mother. *Nik, what are you going to wear?* I posted.

FEMMENIKITA: Surely you jest, XandasAngel. If I went as

anything, it would be as The Blob. Or I could go as a Killer Tomato.

XANDASANGEL: A killer tomato would be cool.

FEMMENIKITA: I should post a reminder to myself to never leave home dressed as a Gigantic Red Fruit. Mother-in-law already tried that when she gave me the most hideous red maternity shirt, size XXL. Do you think she was trying to tell me something?

I thought it was best to be diplomatic, not having any idea what Nik looked like.

XANDASANGEL: Maybe it would look cute.

FEMMENIKITA: That's easy for you to say. You're probably one of those obnoxiously pixielike college girls that look completely normal until you turn sideways.

Which was mostly true, I had to admit, except for the ubiquitous layer of water transforming me from Barbie to the Pillsbury Dough Girl. And the college part.

FEMMENIKITA: Maybe I should go as Where's Waldo, only instead of Waldo, it will be Where's Micah James? Can you find him under all my junk in the trunk? LOL. So what are you and Husband-Who-Can-Do-No-Wrong doing?

A party of course, like any other college student. It didn't occur to me that this lie would be the one to get me into trouble.

FemmeNikita: You owe us pictures. No more of this phantom college student stuff. Everyone at that party is going to have a cell phone with a camera. We're not speaking to you again unless you give us a picture. No excuses.

XandasAngel: I'll try.

I kept telling myself I wanted to go to that party because I needed to get a picture for Nik. But it was more than that.

In art class, I pulled Milo's flyer out for a closer inspection. Delaney's initials were scrawled in the corner with a red pen—the key to opening Dylan's door.

Underneath the address and time, the scrabbled shape of a black crow stood out in relief against the white half sheet, an inversion of the white bird in my drawing.

Like a sign left by Xanda, bidding me to follow.

Nineteen

That's how I ended up at Dylan's Halloween party, sneaking out after my parents disappeared for the night. My mission: to get a photo of Kamran and myself, whatever the cost. And maybe something more.

I looked like a cross between Boris and Natasha in Dad's trench and Xanda's raven-haired wig. I found it deep in the passage between our bedrooms, where I had once found Xanda's safety-pin dress. I would have worn it if it fit. Dylan would have recognized me on the spot.

As I fought through the man-eating ivy bordering Dylan's yard, a flash from out of nowhere sent a rush through my veins—a white-faced ghoul bared his teeth in a drunken grin, made more ghoulish by the porch's yellow light bulb. He took my invitation and tossed it into a pile on the grass.

A cluster of assorted witches, vampires, aliens, and leather-clad anorexics too cool for costumes mobbed the rickety porch staircase, exchanging smoke like kisses. Their eyes followed me with smirks of contempt. As I disappeared into the house, I heard one of them say, "Isn't that Miranda *Mathison*? What happened to *her*?" followed by, "*Xanda's* sister? Oh, my God."

The same house where Delaney had brought me long ago was now shrouded in darkness and crowded with people. I recognized some of them, juniors and seniors from Elna Mead, a few Elna Mead graduates and people I'd seen at Chop Suey. The smell—a mixture of alcohol and incense—reminded me of Xanda's hair.

I wove through the living room. When I reached the kitchen, I realized what had drawn me there. Another layer of notes, pictures, and magnets covered the fridge like a palimpsest, but I saw my sister's face peeking out from the cobbled patchwork. With the party whirling around me, I carefully rearranged the layers and slipped the photo into my pocket.

It was crazy, I realized, to hope to see Kamran apart from Delaney. Maybe they were off in some bedroom together, or lurking behind one of the sea of rubber masks. The cell phone swung in my other pocket like a pendulum.

Then I saw Kamran, gazing out over the crowd. Spidery arms sprouted from his shoulders and fangs from his teeth. His eyes didn't rest on me, didn't recognize me under my disguise, though we were standing only a few feet from each other.

I could speak to him—tell him about Lexi, about Delaney's lies. Or if I couldn't speak, I could at least capture him on film. I turned on my phone's camera, held it at arm's length, carefully covered my face with the long, black hair, stepping backward until I sensed his nearness.

Someone squealed as the camera clicked.

Across the room, a group of Q-tips—out of the box and wreaking havoc—laughed boisterously. Their tall, cottony heads knocked against each other. I couldn't help but smile.

I retreated to a corner with my phone and found myself looking at a tiny picture of me, Kamran, and a fly leaping into the spider's arms the moment the picture snapped. I didn't need to worry about Kamran seeing me. He was too busy devouring Delaney.

One of the Q-tips trilled a bit more loudly than the others at the center of the group. I would have recognized Essence anywhere, even with her head swathed in white and wearing faded blue scrubs.

"What's she doing here?" I muttered, mostly to myself.

"They're cool," said a laid-back voice, as if I had been talking to him all along. And I found myself face-to-face with Dylan, our illustrious host, dressed as himself: black tee and beat-up jeans, looking exactly like Delaney but tall and muscular. And all hotness.

"You're Dylan."

"Wait a second." He narrowed his eyes, searching my face. "Don't I know you?"

Maybe it wasn't such a good idea, crossing this threshold. The house was probably full of people who knew Xanda. Even Andre could be here.

"Yes," I said, blushing. "Well, sort of. I hang out with . . . well, I used to hang out with Delaney sometimes."

"Oh, right. Right." He was still staring, unsatisfied, looking through the long black hair for a hint of the real me. "But there's something else. Did we used to . . ." He got a sheepish smile on his face. Then he noticed the slight bulge of my belly, and the smile dropped instantly.

"You know my sister. Or, you knew my sister. Xanda Mathison."

This was unexpected, I could tell. His questioning look transformed into shock and something deeper. Fear? Anger? Then the laid-back expression returned—a door slamming in my face.

"I knew your sister. She was a bitch, what she did to Andre."

It was that Andre's fault. I knew it, even if I didn't want to.

"What are you talking about?" I countered. In a flash, I could picture with crystal clarity the second she walked out the door: the look on her face, Andre putting his arm around her to protect her from my mother's screaming, only to cause her death an hour later. The secret she would never tell me, lost.

"Shit. Never mind. You probably don't even know. You were a kid."

"I know enough," I said. The crowd around us was getting closer and louder in the dark room, threatening to suffocate me. "I know he was drinking and his driving killed her."

It still hurt to say it. It felt impossible to reconcile what my parents told me with what I knew of Andre. He brought me stuffed animals and candy bars and didn't call me "Blandy" or "Brat" or any of the other names Xanda had officially dubbed me. None of Xanda's boyfriends had ever been like that.

"Damn it." Dylan was looking away, anywhere but at me. "I don't even want to get into this with you." He muttered something I couldn't quite hear over the din of the party. An unholy trio of witches pushed past us, saturating the air with the fresh, gritty odor of cigarettes. Dylan leaned in closer to me to shout into my ear, "I'll tell you this: Things didn't go down the way you think. With Andre. Ask your parents. Hell, don't ask your parents. They've been lying to you all along. You should just ask *him*. He should be here any minute."

A sparkling green fairy followed in the witches' wake, standing on her tiptoes to look over the crowd. She squealed Dylan's name, spreading her arms low and wide and pressing her hand into my stomach to clear the way for giving him a flirtatious smack.

It might have been temporary insanity, but all I could think about was protecting Lexi from the hand pushing into me and the mountain of anger rumbling and choking me with its force—at Dylan, for not telling me what the hell he was talking about. At my parents, for the secrets they were keeping.

At Xanda, for dying, and for leaving me with the fallout. At Andre, for whatever he did or didn't do to make it so. And most especially at the fairy. The blood pounded in my brain, my stomach still grinding from the smoke and churning with this new threat, and the rage bubbled over with one, singular thought in my mind: *How. Dare. You.*

And it probably was insanity, when I caught sight of Delaney standing on a chair and hugging Kamran to her hip. I forced all of the strength and rage into shoving that fairy away from Lexi. She fell backward into the crowd, as if she were an extension of Dylan, my parents, Andre, and Delaney, who shouted, "Oh my God, Rand!" as the fairy flailed her arms, caught by Hellboy and a *Fight Club* reject, guys I thought I recognized from our algebra class last year but who suddenly looked a lot bigger and meaner. They helped the little fairy to her feet and I saw who it was behind the green sparkles and wings: Chloe, looking shocked and wounded and like I hadn't shoved her body but her soul.

I stupidly wanted to explain to Dylan that I hadn't meant to spoil his party or cause a scene. That I wasn't this person who would push someone—a friend—virtually unprovoked. And he must have seen this in my eyes, a hesitation, so he yelled, "Get out! Just get out!" while Chloe leaned on him for support and looked at me with those sad, brown eyes. Several of the Q-tips tittered, "Catfight!" while two of them batted their heads together like swords. Delaney pushed through the crowd to get to Chloe—or maybe to kill me—and was saying,

"You had better start running now," with Kamran's face as unreadable as a black hole. Dylan's voice bit at my heels, "You're as crazy as your sister!" As I pushed my way through the crowd, I knew if I didn't escape *right now,* I would never find my way again.

Eyes of my classmates followed me out of the house, a thousand darts of condemnation. I had shoved Chloe, the most harmless person in the universe. I wouldn't have blamed Delaney for chasing me out the door and taking me out. Chloe was crying.

And I thought I was going to fall down the stairs, or somebody was going to push me, when a cloaked figure moved into the space between me and the concrete below, and I was grateful for a warm body who would keep me and Lexi from pitching to our deaths on Dylan's sidewalk. When he looked up, those eyes connected with mine and a chill of recognition shot through me like a lightning rod in my spine.

"Andre," I said.

"Yeah. Do I know you?"

Oh, God, he didn't recognize me. He couldn't see Xanda in my face, or the grief he'd etched with his own hand.

Or did he?

I didn't respond. My mouth was already numb. I pushed past him, past the boy I still couldn't shake from my memory, away from the party and into the night.

Twenty

I remember the day Dad brought him home.

Dad never brought workers by the house. You couldn't trust those boys, Mom said, with their leering eyes and hands that were never clean, wandering into the bathrooms or the office or the bedroom and leaving a trail of construction dust, taking God knows what. Jewelry. Bank statements. Your daughter's virginity, if you let them.

I guess Dad thought Andre was different. Maybe that's why he brought him across the threshold and into the orbit of our family. Close enough to touch our things. Touch us.

He was seventeen, I think, when he started working for Dad. They stopped by the house on the way to some job in our neighborhood. Dad wanted to grab a ginger ale and a nail gun. Andre had to use the bathroom.

I saw him first.

And I never would have told Xanda, but I loved him first, too.

Two men's voices murmured downstairs. A door slammed shut. Rattling in the kitchen. Mom was out, having left us with strict instructions to finish our homework before she got home. Of course I was the dutiful one, wrestling with a research paper and word problems. Xanda was busy with an old copy of *Jane* magazine, dissecting anything with DIY potential and rifling through her supplies. "A star's got to have style," she'd say.

Xanda wasn't talking to me again. In my twelve years, I had learned to live with her ups and downs.

Another slam, and curiosity got the better of me. I crept to the balcony Dad had designed to overlook the hall opening into the kitchen and family room.

And there he was—young enough to be a possibility, but old enough to be a complete enigma.

He was standing around with Dad, drinking soda in the kitchen. *It was a hot day*, Dad protested later. *I couldn't just leave him in the truck.*

The boy was almost as tall as Dad, but with a wiry, slim build. The better to reach into tight corners, said Dad. The better to evade the border guards, Mom would say. His skin was creamy, but with a layer of brownness from working outside. Black hair, with a curious tint of blue in the light. Wearing boots and torn-up jeans with a chain stretching from pocket to waist, a well-worn T-shirt featuring a cartoon piece of toast chasing a pat of butter. Odd.

Oddly appealing. Especially when his face turned toward mine and he smiled a huge, bright smile, pretty much stopping my twelve-year-old heart. No one smiled at me like that, like I was the only girl in the universe—or at least the house . . . until his eyes traveled upward, beyond me. I hadn't heard Xanda sneak up. She stood there on the landing, spellbound, as entranced as I was by this mystery Dad brought into our midst. She put her hand on my shoulder, like she needed me to keep her standing. Her hand was shaking. Maybe if I had been closer to him, I might have seen if he was shaking, too.

I was suddenly conscious of the dirty socks I was wearing, and how visible they were under my too-short pants. I was always growing out of my clothes—too tall and skinny to wear Xanda's old ones instead of the dorky ones Mom bought for me. Xanda wore her white peasant blouse, shredded and reconstructed to skim her shape, a skirt that used to be Mom's, but completely transformed into Xanda's signature antistyle, with striped knee-highs. She looked fabulous.

"This is Andre," said my dad, clearly oblivious to the triangle of electricity quickly becoming a line between them.

It was always like this, because Xanda couldn't help but be Xanda, and people couldn't help but be stopped in their tracks by her. This boy, I couldn't blame him. He was about to become the latest in a long string, caught in her irresistible gravity and crushed by its weight. But then something happened.

The boy turned his gaze back to me, and he smiled. An inclusive, charming smile, like the line of electricity between them had opened up. There was room for both of us in that smile.

Then the moment was over, as soon as Dad took a final gulp and slapped Andre on the back. "Let's hit the road."

In a flash, Xanda was doing what I could only imagine, running down the stairs to waylay them with some pretense—anything that would keep the blue-hued boy from walking away forever. I leaned over the rail to watch. As Xanda would say, *Watch and learn*.

"Are you working on the Hanson project?" she asked Dad. The Hanson house was just over the ridge, on the view side of the hill. Trey Hanson was in the class above mine and was well known for torturing small animals and me, until Xanda threatened to kick his ass last summer if he didn't leave me alone. He never bothered me again.

"Yup," said Dad. "We're installing the hardwood today. You two girls want to come help? I think I've got an extra mallet around."

"Uh, no thanks, just wondered. How late you gonna be there?"

"I'll be home for dinner. Can you order pizza or something before your mom gets home? Or," he said, raising his voice to me, "we could get Mandy to cook again. That spaghetti you made last night was pretty good." I blushed at the compliment. Maybe someday I'd be making spaghetti for Andre, too.

They left, and I headed back to my homework while

Xanda went to her room. Her lock snapped shut, but through the passage, I could hear her singing her favorite Splashdown song.

And later that night, after the sun had set, I looked out my window and saw Xanda slip through the shadows in a swishy red halter dress, her hair whipping behind her as she hurried to meet her date—and maybe her destiny.

Every night after, she slipped out to meet the boy, Andre, at the end of our block. I came to recognize the rumble of his green Impala as the days grew shorter and the nights colder, and Mom dove deeper into the Christmas montage and Dad into his work. The only thing left was me, trying to hold all of them together.

The office light was on when I drove up our street. Mom working late, or maybe Dad settling some accounts. The bars on the office window—left over from when it was still Xanda's bedroom—were white in the daylight, practically unobtrusive. In the dark, it looked like an eye with great, rigid lashes. By the time they installed the bars, it had been far too late.

It felt strange to be seeing the house as Xanda so often did, on the night my life might have been swapped for hers.

Nik would say you had to walk in someone else's shoes to understand the path they were on. My mother thought my path should be straight. She couldn't begin to imagine me following the turns of Xanda's life.

If I really wanted to walk Xanda's road, I would have shimmied up the maple tree and the trellis, but I doubted they would bear my weight now. Lexi had been in enough danger already this evening, so I opted for the front door.

I was crossing into my bedroom when light flooded the hallway. It was Mom, with her hair down and dressed in her nightgown.

"Hi, honey," she yawned, sleep overtaking the usual hard edges of her voice.

"You're probably wondering why I was out." I hadn't prepared anything. Even in her nightgown, my mom could detonate at any moment.

But the impact never came. In the glow from Xanda's old bedroom, my mother looked almost vulnerable, like someone I could trust. "No, I'm not," she sighed. And I could feel my guard beginning to drop.

I stood on the edge of telling her everything, and asking what really happened to Xanda.

Until she spoke.

"I went through this with your sister, and now I'm going through it with you." Her eyes were sharpened, like splintered glass. "To tell you the truth, this time maybe I'd rather not know."

She left me there, speechless. Alone with my memories of the party, Andre, and another dead end.

Twenty-one

Where my pregnancy made a mere ripple in the Elna Mead ecosystem, the fallout from Dylan's party turned out to be massive. Suddenly I was a one-woman episode of *Girls Gone Wild*—first my pregnancy, then my shocking attempt to trap Kamran, then my brutal treatment of Chloe, who at five-foot-two stood a full six inches shorter than me and couldn't possibly stand up to my bullying.

I felt even worse when I found Chloe's email in my in-box the next morning—"This is Friendship Week, and I'm glad you're my friend!" Sent right before the Halloween party.

Ty Belkin bumped me in the hall and apologized loudly: "Oops. Sorry, Rand. I thought you were Chloe." Pretty soon everybody was bumping me with the same excuse—except for freshmen, who gave me a wide berth and were content whispering *I heard she's psycho*, and *I heard her sister was psycho, too.*

Delaney was in her element, relating the scandal to a fresh wave of disciples: "I had no idea she was *like* that. But then I should have known—even her best friend Essence doesn't talk to her anymore. I mean, I feel sorry for her, after her sister died and everything. But still." Chloe stood by, basking in the avalanche of sympathy. Kamran looked pained, my existence a glitch in the pattern of his life.

Even Essence's status rose among the general populace—no longer Cross Your Heart, she was now Victim with the Inside Scoop. People who never would have noticed Essence before were lining up to get the story. She tried to catch my attention as I strode past—to rub it in or to offer pity? I didn't need either one.

With French fries and root-beer milk shakes, I bribed Mrs. Crooker to write passes for my other classes, supposedly to finish my portfolio. I still had to face period after period of art students, but at least she kept them too busy to bother me. Maybe she had heard. Maybe she felt sorry for me. Maybe she remembered my sister and hoped I wouldn't end up the same way.

So my parents' ultimatum might have seemed like a blessing—if it hadn't come attached to a curse.

Ever since my mom caught me after the Halloween party, I'd been waiting for the other shoe to drop. Bars on my window, grounded for life, cutting off all communication . . . any one of them might have been better than having to go to the first montage rehearsal and watch Essence arrive with a carload of the drama crowd, laughing and then going serious when she saw me. Her lines echoed in my head as if they were mine, only she played the good daughter while my mom nodded her head in approval.

At least when I got home, I could hide in my room to work on my drawings. I had tucked the stolen picture of Xanda into my sketchbook, sandwiched between the labyrinths as a reference for my portraits. It was a window. A clue.

Mom and I were driving home from practice the week after the party when she cleared her throat. "Your dad and I have been talking . . ."

I braced for impact.

". . . and we've decided to enroll you in the work-study program at school. Your dad has arranged for a paid internship at First Washington Credit Union doing some accounting . . ."

"*Accounting?*" This was so out of left field, I couldn't even believe what I was hearing.

"It's a great program," my mom continued. "You go to the work-study class right after your lunch period, then you go to the bank for training every day. On Fridays, you'll go straight from work to rehearsals. You start next week."

"But I have my art class in the afternoons!"

Mom sighed, infinitely patient. "I know this isn't what you want, Mandy. But the reality is, what you want is no longer possible. We're trying to help you. You're having a baby. You should be grateful we're not kicking you out."

"But a *bank*?" This conversation was only going downhill. "What about art school? I thought you said you wanted me to be a teacher."

Her voice dripped with cold, common sense. "I'm sorry, Miranda, but you've got to be practical, and you can't afford to spend four years in school plus a teaching-prep program—because you're having a baby now. We're not going to be there to pick up the pieces. You can still do your art when you're not working." She snorted, "Or taking care of the baby, which is going to be a lot more work than you—"

"But *Mom*—"

"Art school would be fine if you had a few years to play around before settling into your career, but you don't have that luxury anymore."

"I'm not *playing around*. I'm serious about my art." She didn't understand. It's what I was meant to do.

"You've made some poor decisions"—we pulled into the driveway at a crazy angle, and the car stopped with a jerk—"and your father and I are trying to help you get back on track. If you're going to keep this baby, we're not going to be able to support your art school plans."

What?

Shock and outrage flooded me, but all I could seem to do was squeak out a whine. "Why not? What difference does it make?"

"It makes a big difference. First, you're going to expect us to pay for college. Then you're going to expect *me* to take care of the baby. Next thing you know, you're going to be off doing God knows what with your artist boyfriends and getting yourself killed—"

Like Xanda.

"—then where will this baby be? Without a mother *or* father, and we get stuck with the bill?" Her voice rose to a familiar tone. She slammed the car into park. "If you have any shred of unselfishness, you'll give this baby up to a family who is capable of caring for it. If you keep it, you're condemning it to a life of misery. I can't believe you would be that selfish."

You mean condemning you, I thought.

"On the other hand, if you give up the baby, you could still pursue your art." Under her breath, she added, "We can only hope you will decide to pursue a more stable career later."

I couldn't believe this was happening. Was she really trying to force me to give up Lexi? *How did Xanda and I ever come out of you?* I wanted to scream. All she cared about was looking perfect. Even if I said the words, I knew she wouldn't hear them.

"You can either keep the baby or go to art school. The choice is yours."

I couldn't wait to find Nik online. I didn't even care about keeping up my college-student story. She could know everything there was to know about me, every hideous truth I'd ever tried to hide. *Ugly or not, Nik, here I come.*

I hadn't seen her online since before Halloween. Maybe she was visiting her stepson, who lived a few hours away. She was bound to be back by now.

I logged on to the BabyCenter board, and a feeling of dread swept over me. Entry after entry began, "Nik, I am so sorry." Or, "Nik, I can't believe this happened to you." The chat room was silent.

I scrolled back through the day's posts and found hers, posted by FemmeNikita at 9:32 this morning:

I'm writing to tell all of you how much it has meant to me to have your friendship and support through this sweetest time of my life.

Last week, I started cramping and bleeding. My husband rushed me to the hospital, where I delivered our baby at twenty-three weeks, too early for him to survive. Even at less than a pound, he was the most beautiful thing I have ever seen. We named him Micah James. I won't forget his tiny fingers and toes, or the way he fit in the palm of my husband's hand. I have never seen my husband weep as he wept over our little boy.

Our hearts are broken. But faith always manages. I won't be posting anymore on this board, as it is painful to hear about your pregnancies when we have lost one so precious to us. I hold you all in my heart and wish you joy.

Faith. The future. A life without Micah James.

My own crisis suddenly seemed so small.

That night I lay in bed, the images of Lexi replaying in my mind like a window into another world. I tried to recapture the wonder of her profile—tiny chin, nub of nose, round skull with two hemispheres of brain beneath. Ten fingers, ten toes, a spine rippling with tiny bones. Small enough to fit in the palm of my hand.

I lay on my back like the ob-gyn said, waiting to feel a flutter.

I had nearly slipped into unconsciousness when I did feel something, like a bubble popping. A gurgle. I wondered if it was just gas. I poked my belly where I felt it and waited.

The bubble popped again, a tap of recognition.

Nineteen weeks after we had started this journey together, Lexi and I shared our first communiqué—a secret Morse code between passenger and host.

Twenty-two

My parents wasted no time setting me on the path to banking glory. I completely bypassed the application and interview process for my cushy new job at First Washington Credit Union, filing and processing checks in the secretarial dungeon and occasionally filling in for a teller.

No doubt they expected the job to be so terrible, I'd make the call to Social Services myself—and I might have, if I hadn't just read about Nik and felt Lexi for the first time. I wasn't about to lose her or my dream. *Money in the bank,* as Dad would say. Lexi and I would need it.

I'd been in the credit union a thousand times before, but it's funny how you notice details when your cell door is about to slam and lock—like the carpet coming undone in the middle

of the room, or the slightly mismatched square by the loans
desk. Or the scowl on the loan officer's face under a mop of
fat dreadlocks as she watched my mom and me walk through
the revolving doors. Carefully she extricated herself from
the desk and shambled toward us. She shot a glance toward
one of the tellers, who immediately hustled to the loans desk.
The others rearranged themselves to fill the gap like the Von
Trapp Family tellers.

I struggled to arrange my new shirt and pants.

As usual, I had gone through my closet about fifty times
yesterday. Desperate and close to tears, I'd crawled into the
passage to check Xanda's boxes for something—babydoll
dress? Poncho? Anything. I nearly crashed into my mother as
she came into the office, my face a red, puffy dam.

"What's this about?"

Just pick something, I thought. Instead, I sniffed, "Nothing."
We did a little dance in the hall, her capturing and me trying
to escape.

"I was looking for something in . . . the passage."

"Why do you want to get into Xanda's things?" Her eyes
narrowed as she took me in—red eyes, skanked-out hair, my
low jeans and the hem of my sweater grazing my newly outed,
and extremely touchy, belly button. The light of dawn spread
across her face.

"I see. Well, I guess we're just going to have to go shopping
then."

She smiled—like this was a peace offering, after trading

art school for banking hell.

A half hour and a rainstorm later, we were cruising through the mall in search of The Well-Heeled Mother. Though it could have been The Well-Heeled Grandmother. When I started to look through a rack of cute sheer tops, Mom steered me to the "much more practical" round of striped button-ups and stretchy black slacks.

The salesgirl, perky and looking ready to pop herself, sidled up to my mom. "We've got some great new winter arrivals. Are you the lucky mama?"

"No," glowered Mom.

The clue gun missed, and the girl turned to me. "You?"

I nodded.

Back to Mom: "So you must be the proud grandmother. Is this your first?"

"*Yes.*" Though she looked anything but proud, with me hunting through a rack of enormous, tent-shaped tops.

"Congratulations! Let me show you our basics—great for work, or"—the salesgirl shot an unsure look at me—"er, school, or . . . *whatever.*"

Before I could say "muumuu," I had a stack of clothes in a dressing room with two "bellies"—pillows I could strap around myself to see what I might look like in a few more months. I put on one of the shirts—a red one, like Nik's Killer Tomato shirt.

She wouldn't be needing it now.

After hours of mother-daughter retail bonding, we finally

emerged with a nonrefundable bag of the most unflattering clothes I would ever wear. But at least I would *have* something to wear, Mom reminded me.

We had almost escaped the mall when I spotted an Elna Mead group at the sushi bar next to Guess. They hadn't spotted me, probably because I looked like a well-heeled grandmother now.

And that's when Essence's voice said brightly, "Hi, Rand. Hi, Mrs. Mathison."

My mom stopped dead in her tracks, and I had no choice but to follow suit. It was still pouring down rain, and she was the one holding the keys.

"What are you doing here?" Essence asked. Like we weren't allowed to go to the mall or something.

"Just out to do some shopping," Mom said, waving our bag.

"Wow, you're getting *huge*." Exactly the kind of observation I could always count on from Essence.

"I'm not huge," I muttered. "I'm almost five months pregnant."

"She didn't mean anything, Mandy," my mother growled. Mom defending Essence—that was a first. Must be their chummy new relationship, now that Essence had stepped into the role of Brenda the Perfect. "She's tired," Mom explained. "Pregnancy, schoolwork . . ."

"Yeah," I cut in, "and starting tomorrow, I have that job you got for me since I can't go to art school anymore."

Even Essence was taken aback. "You're not going to art school?" Of anyone, she would understand exactly what art school meant to me.

"No, because *somebody* has to support this baby," I parroted, "and it won't be a starving artist." I could see my mom getting increasingly uncomfortable with this line of conversation. Essence was right. Revenge could be fun. "Besides," I added, "even art school isn't worth giving up the baby."

"So," Mom said, giving me the death stare, "Essence. About that Cornish recommendation letter—I'll get it to you in the next few days. You've made some really incredible strides as an actor this year. I've been really impressed."

I was too stunned to respond. *A letter of recommendation? For Cornish College of the Arts?* Essence went back to gushing, completely oblivious to my mom's conversation coup.

Essence was prattling about the *Guys and Dolls* tryouts coming up, but I was somewhere between hurt and rage. Did she spill my secret just to get brownie points? This was about getting on my mom's good side? Suddenly my memory shifted, the details in sharp relief—like her car spinning out of Milo's driveway, a phone call away from ruining my life.

So now, as the dread-head bank manager woman ambled toward me, some of that meekness stuck with me as I tugged my pants and shirt into place, unconsciously smoothing the tummy that had gone from fat to pregnant in one, unexpected pop.

The woman finally reached us and locked eyes with me. "Shelley Jones. Manager. Follow me," she said.

"Well, I can't stay," my mom twittered, "I have to get to—"

"Oh," Shelley Jones said, "I'm sorry. Are you working here, too? I was under the impression it was only your daughter."

Whoa. I was instantly impressed. And the tiniest bit terrified.

"Well," said my mother. She looked more flustered than I had ever seen her. "I'll be back to pick you up at six, then."

"Make it six forty-five. We don't leave when the customers do."

"Oh. Of course. Six forty-five, then." And my mom was out the door, leaving me to face Shelley alone. I followed her timidly to a windowed office in the back corner of the building. Plum-colored metal blinds fit floor to ceiling in the windows, sealed as if for an interrogation. She closed the solid wood door behind me and shuffled around the desk to an office chair clearly designed to accommodate her considerable weight.

"Wow, that was incredible—"

"So, you're the pregnant girl I had to hire. Mandy."

"Rand."

"Rand. Apparently I'm supposed to reform you." I was still standing there, unsure whether to stand or sit. She gave me the once-over, lingering for a moment on my newly striped belly.

"What would you rather be doing besides banking? And don't tell me hanging out with your boyfriend, because I really

141

don't want to hear about that."

I knew I looked like the village idiot, staring with my mouth open, but I really had no idea how to respond. I mean, I'd never been around anybody so . . . direct before. My family didn't operate that way.

Shelley leaned her head in closer. "I asked you a question. Are you impaired in some way that you are unable to answer my question?" She was completely deadpan as she said this, her eyes round and huge.

"I'm sorry," I stammered, "I mean, no, I don't have a boyfriend. Not anymore."

"Of course not. So now that the boyfriend is no longer in the picture, and you graduate this year, what were you planning to do?"

"Art," I said, proud of myself for finally forming a straight answer. "I mean, I'm an artist."

"So banking is the worst thing your parents could think of to punish you for being pregnant."

That pretty much summed it up, didn't it? So I simply said, "Yes." And then I kind of felt bad for my parents and added, "Though they just want me to be able to support the baby since I decided to keep it."

She raised one eyebrow, the effect near petrifying. "And what made you decide to keep it?"

I thought about telling her about Xanda, about the path I'd been tracing, how this baby would be the bird, the escape, the thing to change everything. But instead I blurted, "It was my parents. My parents wanted me to give it up. I wanted to keep her from the beginning."

"So you got pregnant on purpose?" Again, the deadpan face. I didn't think I could get used to this.

"No!" That, I was sure about. "No, it just happened. It was an accident."

"Right," she said, like she didn't quite believe me. "So. Back to banking. Can I assume you are planning to dedicate yourself to learning the banking trade? Or are you going to be daydreaming about art and babies all day long?"

Of course I would be thinking about art and my baby. But I would try. That was all she could expect from me. "I'll do my best," I said.

The rest of the afternoon, Shelley Jones dedicated herself to teaching me the fine art of banking grunt work.

Twenty-three

Throughout November, I performed a bevy of soul-sucking tasks for Shelley, who quickly decided my top banking talent was destroying sensitive financial documents.

"You can think about art and that boyfriend all you want, cozying up to the shredder," she said.

I had to gulp back a "Yes, sir."

Not that I wanted to learn banking from the inside out, but she could at least give me a chance. Any time I strayed from shredding, her door would swing wide and she would give me that look. It kept me shredding four days a week.

When I wasn't shredding, I went to Christmas montage practice or church on Sundays with barely enough time for homework and sleep. Everything else faded, including the

BabyCenter girls. There wasn't much to say, now that Nik was gone.

"You're still applying to Baird, aren't you?" Mrs. Crooker asked when I told her my art class had been replaced by the work-study program. I didn't tell her my parents had pulled the plug on art school. I had time, I thought. Applications, financial aid . . . there had to be time to change the direction of the future.

"Yeah. I just have to finish a couple more drawings." I filled my notebook with sketches of Lexi, of the landscapes inside my mind and body, of Xanda, trying to pick up the trail where I had left off. *Things didn't go down the way you think*, Dylan had said. *Don't ask your parents. They've been lying to you all along.*

The only clue I had for what might have happened was the photograph I stole from Dylan. One Saturday morning, I spent an hour searching every passage and cupboard for a single photo of Xanda in the years before she died. Had Mom destroyed them all? The albums—neatly arranged on the office shelf—had pictures of my parents, of me when I was little, and a few seemingly accidental ones of Xanda as a kid—holding me, in the background, almost an afterthought. Except for an elbow here, a flash of hair there, almost no evidence of her life was left.

As my belly got bigger, so did the moat of space surrounding me at Elna Mead. Delaney and her entourage no longer acknowledged my existence. I wanted to talk to Kamran, but what could I say? About Halloween? About Lexi? He would be knee-deep in his MIT application now, with Harvard as backup—which only made me cling to Baird more, hoping somehow our space-time continuums would collide.

I almost did collide with a swift, tiny blond on my way out of class. I thought she was new until I recognized the brown eyes under a gloss of new highlights.

"Chloe?" Her hair was the same color as Delaney's now, practically twins. She wore a tight black sweater that used to be Delaney's. And before that, it was mine.

"Oh, Rand. Hi." She looked up at me nervously, like I was about to push her over here and now.

"I'm sorry about what happened," I began.

She was looking past me, and I followed her gaze. Delaney waited for her in the main corridor, with a junior Delaney always pointed out as an example of what not to wear. Delaney looked different, too—from naughty to nice, reinvented into the object of Kamran's desire.

"Um, gotta go. See you around," Chloe mumbled before scurrying into the new triumvirate.

"You dumped your best friend for that?"

Voice of my conscience? Hardly. It was Essence.

The shirt she wore—faded maroon, cracked screen printing of a caged bird, brass stitching . . . I remembered the day we went shopping for it, after she had saved her babysitting money to buy something cool to wear to the eighth-grade assembly. We sat together on the front lines hoping Erik Anderssen would notice one of us—it didn't matter which.

Part of me was embarrassed for her, wearing that ratty old T-shirt with jeans, probably dropped off at the thrift store a decade ago along with the navy blue cardigan she wore.

But the other part noticed how different she looked, now that I wasn't seeing her through Delaney's eyes. Pretty, even.

"An apology wouldn't hurt, you know." The whiny edge to her voice was gone. Now it was just cold.

"An apology?"

People walked around us like water navigating the rocks, flowing into the classrooms before the bell rang. No one noticed the geek and the outcast, yesterday's news.

"Yes, an apology. I realize I'm not as cool as Delaney, and I probably never will be. But we were friends, Rand. Do you want to know how I felt when you and Delaney started hanging out? I was happy for you. I was glad to be included, but mostly I was happy for you, because I knew that's what you wanted. I thought maybe it would help you deal with Xanda . . . but it only made you mean."

She waited for me to respond.

I could have taken the path she offered me. Said, "I'm sorry I chose Delaney over you." I wanted to. Ten years of memories pressed me to say the words I'd just said so easily to Chloe. She had been my friend—my dorky, annoying, truthful best friend.

But in a flash, I remembered the look on her face when she peeled away from the party, burning with my secret. She could afford to be nice, now that she had what she wanted.

Lexi reserved most of her kicking for nighttime, but as she shifted, all of the emotions I'd been storing up for months came rushing out. "You paid me back, so maybe we're even now," I said.

"What are you talking about?" The halls were empty now, just her and me standing in the gray light of the corridor.

"How about this?" I gestured toward my stomach as my heart rate picked up speed. Lexi moved, swimming her backstrokes and bumping into the walls of my body. "I've got no boyfriend, no friends, a pregnancy I'm not even sure I want . . . all because you had a big piece of news for the prayer chain."

Essence looked stunned. As if it were some great deduction for me to figure out she'd sent the news from one end of the chain to the other, ending with my mom.

"I may have ditched you, but you decimated me," I continued. "For the lead part? A Cornish reference from my mom? I'd say that was payback. So yeah, I'm sorry we grew apart, and I'm sorry I spilled beer on you at the party, but you didn't have to go tell everyone I was pregnant. I would much rather you said you hated me to my face."

"So would I." Essence looked more sad than angry. "I can't believe you think I would do that. Delaney would do that. Maybe you would do that, but not me. In a way I'm glad you did what you did, because now I know what kind of a person you are. I don't need that." As she talked, her voice caught. She blinked tears away. "I can get my own parts, thank you very much. I didn't need to hurt you for people to notice me. If you want to know who told your mom, try asking your supposed *friends.*"

My mind hooked on a memory: *You told him?* I asked. *Of course not, but Essence . . . I think she heard us talking. . . .*

"I've gotta get to drama class. Tryouts for *Guys and Dolls* are next week."

With a quick wipe of her navy-blue sleeve, she pushed past me and sped down the hall to the theater. I was left to wonder if I had made a terrible, terrible mistake.

"Good luck," I said after her. But she was already gone.

Twenty-four

"I don't think I'll be here for Thanksgiving," I announced to my parents after montage practice. After watching Mom direct Essence and the other actors as the ideal family for the last two hours, I just wanted to give thanks alone.

"Oh?" said my dad, not taking his eyes off of his soup.

Mom continued picking through her pad Thai. "And where do you plan to be?"

My options were limited. School cafeteria? The FWCU break room? Under the University Bridge? "Well," I lied, "Delaney is getting together a bunch of people from school to serve dinner down at the teen homeless shelter, and I thought you wouldn't mind . . ."

In reality, Delaney and her dad would be giving thanks *à*

la mode française at Rover's, the most exclusive French place in town—no doubt with Chloe in tow.

Essence would be having Thanksgiving and all the trimmings with her parents, grandparents, and as many relatives as her mom could cram into their two-bedroom Cape Cod–style house, thankful to be rid of me.

And Kamran . . . since Big Boss would be closed for the holiday, maybe he would be home, eating Persian turkey pilaf, preparing for his visit to the MIT campus. Or maybe he would be with Delaney, too.

My father raised his eyebrows. "I haven't seen Delaney around much lately. I thought, after the pregnancy . . ." He trailed off, probably not wanting to mess with my tender hormonal state. "Glad I was wrong."

"Marvelous." Mom smiled, seemingly forgetting she'd been the one to ground me for life. "We can make a pie Thursday morning for you to take."

Mom wasn't much of a cook, but she could make a killer pie crust. She insisted on making two pies: one for the shelter, and the other for her and Dad to eat with the tofu-turkey she was going to try her hand at baking, complete with instant mashed potatoes, canned cranberries, and a side of microwaved peas. I was almost proud of my kitchen-challenged mother.

If I was going to eat this pie under a bridge, it had better be fresh pumpkin, not canned. I scraped the cooked pumpkin out of the skin into a bowl alongside Mom, both of us quiet except for my spoon against the pumpkin's flesh and the *poof* of flour as Mom dropped a cup into the mixing bowl. It was the first time in weeks that we'd been in the same room together without rehearsals or traffic drowning out the discomfort.

"How are things at school?" she asked, never taking her eyes off of the bowl as she measured and sifted the flour.

"Fine." Scrape.

"And work?"

"Good." Scrape.

She pressed the dough into the pie pan while I stirred up the pumpkin, sugar, spices, and condensed milk. There was more waiting behind her eyes as she watched me stir.

I mustered up one of the yawns always at the ready—extreme fatigue brought about by the real and exhausting task of creating another human being. "I should rest before I go. I'm pretty tired, after working and the play and everything." It felt good, doling out a dollop of guilt.

Later, as I gathered up the pie and headed out into the rain, it occurred to me I really could go to Kamran's. Maybe I could crash the party and munch on dates with Mr. and Mrs. Ziyal as we discussed the future of their grandchild. They probably hadn't heard the news.

If I were Xanda, I might have done it.

As I drove, I considered the options: Bridge. Church. Crash Kamran's. Crash the French restaurant. The bridge idea wasn't so bad, except for the homeless guys who would be as hungry for a piece of me as for the pie. Plus, I forgot to bring a fork.

Luckily, First Washington was at the next stoplight, and I had my key.

I rolled into the bank lot. I could just stay here and find some hot tea, and maybe take a nap on the lobby couch. The building was dark, deserted on one of the few bank holidays of the year. Even the parking lot was empty. Nobody would be out in the rain when they could be inside watching football or Thanksgiving reruns, feasting on turkey and family love.

Just then, a black SUV pulled up beside me, blurred by the droplets on my windows—on a candied-yam run, or needing cash to contribute to the communal turkey. The windshield and windows were dark.

The driver didn't make a move. No one got out of the passenger side. A bubble of worry formed in my chest. I stayed still, tilting my face away to avoid recognition. In a flash, I could see myself being dragged out of the car, my pie-weapon falling pitifully onto the pavement. I was helpless to protect Lexi, if someone really wanted to hurt me. I could hear myself formulating the sentence that had been in my mind since the day I saw the ultrasound: *If you hurt my baby, I will kill you.* I would use a pie plate, a cigarette lighter, even push Chloe. I turned the key and started my engine.

As I backed out of the parking space, a body jumped out of the SUV and lunged toward my passenger window. I froze. A hand knocked on the window, a face peered out of a hooded ski jacket. Round eyes locked with mine. I felt like I would shatter with relief, and then with fear, caught in the bank parking lot.

It was Shelley, my boss.

She pounded on the window. "Are you okay?" Drizzle from the rolled-down window was getting dangerously close to my Thanksgiving dinner, perched on the passenger seat.

"Yeah," I shouted, "I'm fine." I moved the pie away from the rain, and she took it as an invitation to get in.

"I came by to pick up my laptop, and you're sitting out here in the rain. What are you doing here? Where are your parents? Are you headed somewhere?" She took one look at my pie, and one at my belly, and one at what must have been a pretty pathetic face.

"You don't have anywhere to go, do you." It was more of a statement than a question. "And you were going to sit there and eat your pie, feeling sorry for yourself."

"No, I have somewhere to go," I protested. "It's just that—"

"It's just that you're coming to my house instead, right?"

"I am?"

"Because I'm not going to let you sit here with that beautiful pie going to waste here in this bank parking lot. Pumpkin?"

I nodded.

"Then come on, park your car and we'll go. And don't forget to bring that pie with you."

Twenty-five

I climbed into Shelley's SUV and saw a whole new way of looking at the world. Up high, fearless, with places to go.

Twenty minutes later, we parked in front of a navy-blue and lime-green Victorian house near Green Lake. It towered above us from a foundation of mossy rocks, overshadowed by an even taller cedar. Needles and cones littered the sidewalk and parking strip below.

"Watch your step," Shelley ordered as we threaded our way up the narrow, careening steps. "These old houses were not exactly built to code." She offered me her hand as I tested each step, balancing the pie in my other hand.

A boy about six years old burst through the front door, throwing himself around Shelley's waist. "What took you so long? We been waiting for you all day." He gave her one mean frown, then spotted me. "Who's that?"

I felt like I always did in the presence of kids: off balance, not quite sure how to approach.

Shelley laughed, a low, hearty laugh that took me by surprise. "I went to get my laptop, but I came home with a stray. So I guess I won't be getting any work done this weekend." I could imagine Shelley being the workaholic at home as well as at the bank. I wasn't so sure I could buy into this softer side, taking in strays and mothering this small boy. "Rand, this is DaShawn. DaShawn, this is Rand."

The boy was still giving me the once-over, and I was glad to have the pie in hand. I passed it to him. "This is for you." His eyes went as round as chocolate kisses while his nose took in the squashy aroma up close and personal.

"For everybody," Shelley shouted as he took off running into the house with the pie. "Good move," she said to me. "The way to his heart is through pumpkin pie."

A cloud of warmth hit me as we walked into Shelley's house. Her husband, a wiry guy with the energy of a middle schooler, bounded out of the kitchen with a phone against his ear. He hung up and started to take our coats as he said to Shelley, "Thank God you're finally home, because I think I've pretty much burned this turkey to a crisp."

"How can you burn something in an oven bag?" Shelley demanded, taking her coat off and showing me in. "And incidentally, this is our guest, Rand. I found her outside the bank with a pumpkin pie. Rand, this is my husband, James."

"She's a stray," said DaShawn, who looked decidedly disappointed when his dad scooped the pumpkin pie out of his grasp. "Aw, *man*."

"Later." James gave him a mock-warning look. To me, he said, "Nice to meet you, Stray Rand."

"Just Rand, thanks." I gave Shelley a questioning look. "Are you sure I'm not intruding on your Thanksgiving?"

"And where were you planning to go if you were? You forget, you left your car at the bank."

"So you're stuck here," said James. "Do you generally hang out in the bank parking lot, or is this just a Thanksgiving thing?"

I could feel the blush rising. Maybe this wasn't such a great idea after all.

"Give her a break, James," Shelley said pointedly. "She's not used to you picking on her all the time." As if Shelley didn't pick on me enough.

"Not like you, huh, baby." He gave her a noisy smooch.

I didn't need to see my boss and her hubby kissing in the kitchen, even though it was almost a welcome change from the frigid waters of home. I dramatically smacked my hands over my eyes and shouted, "Ewwwww! TMI, people! TMI!"

Shelley rolled her eyes. DaShawn said, "What's TMI?" And James suddenly remembered to check the turkey.

"Too much information," I whispered to DaShawn. He raised his eyebrow knowingly.

"Great," drawled Shelley. "That's all he needs—more ammunition."

Fifteen minutes later we were all crammed into their olive-colored dining room, trying to avoid spilling green beans and gravy onto the tomato-red tablecloth, which looked like it had seen its share of mealtime battles—especially on DaShawn's side of the table.

"Make sure you put a lot of gravy on that turkey. It's dry as a piece of week-old toast." Shelley loaded DaShawn's plate with food as James made a huge production out of slicing the turkey at the head of the table. Norman Rockwell turkey, it was not. Out of the bag and on the platter, the turkey looked more like it was headed for the fossil museum. Even gravy couldn't save it.

"What do you think, Rand?" James held the electric knife aloft, so it didn't exactly seem like a good idea to insult his handiwork.

"Um, it looks great," I mumbled. "Mmmm. Smells delicious."

"See." He puffed up, giving the electric knife another rev in Shelley's direction. "I told you Turkey Talk was a good idea."

"You called Turkey Talk?" I sputtered. They'd been advertising Turkey Talk all week, the "turkey helpline" sponsored by one of the local TV stations. No one in my family would ever call Turkey Talk, no matter how bad my mom's cooking could be.

DaShawn sawed away at his meat, singing, "Don't know

what to dooo-hooo when Turkey Day finds yoooou-hooo? Call Turkey Talk, *yeah*, *yeah*, call Turkey Talk!"

"Oh, Lord," said Shelley.

"How did you think I managed to cook this magnificent bird?" James continued to chainsaw off hunks of parched meat and stacked it high on the platter, the mirror image of DaShawn: big twin and little twin. "Rand likes it."

"Well . . . ," I started, and he gave me that same mean frown I'd gotten from DaShawn as I came through the door.

"Now wait one minute. I thought you were my ally." To DaShawn: "Guess it's just you and me, buddy."

"Whatever, Dad." And DaShawn was back to his Turkey Talk jingle as we finished our dinner and then cleaned up the kitchen.

Neither Shelley nor I said much on the drive back, making the journey seem surreal after the chaos of her house.

"I really liked your son," I ventured. "He looks a lot like his dad."

"He's his dad's son, that's for sure. Both of them trouble-makers. I wish we could have him more often."

"More often? Doesn't he live with you?"

"He lives with his mom, but we get him every other weekend and some holidays. We get him for Thanksgiving and even Christmas this year."

"Doesn't that bother you?"

"Faith manages." I waited for her to say more, but the silence stretched out into the stop-and-go city traffic, like I'd said exactly the wrong thing. If only life came with an "undo" button, I would undo what I'd said.

Undo the Christmas montage disaster. Undo what I'd done to Essence, and what Delaney had done to me. Undo meeting Kamran. Undo Xanda's death.

Undo Lexi?

No. She was my chance to make everything right.

Twenty-six

Elna Mead scheduled the Winter Ball for the last weekend before the holiday break—as if planning for the biggest commercial season wasn't enough, they had to add the biggest mackfest of the year.

It was hard to walk—or in my case, waddle—through the hall without overhearing people bragging about their dates ("Cole asked me! Finally!") or their dresses ("Well, my mom wanted me to go to Nordstrom, but I told her I *had* to have the Betsey Johnson one . . .") or the hopes of scoring ("Latiesha! Right on."), accompanied by the appropriate hand-slapping and high-fiving.

Delaney joined the Winter Ball planning efforts, the last stage of her transformation from bad girl to prom queen. She and Chloe marched through the halls with staple guns and posters for maximum marketing effectiveness to the glitterati of Elna Mead High—as well as those she couldn't quite ban from the event. Like Essence. Or me.

Not that she really needed to worry about either one of us. The Winter Ball coincided every year with the opening night of the Christmas montage. After that, I would go back to my job at First Washington, and Essence would be immersed in *Guys and Dolls* rehearsals. I scanned the cast list, beginning at the bottom. My eyes had nearly reached the top when they rested on her name: *Essence Hannah . . . Adelaide*. Her dream role, the limelight she deserved.

At home behind the scenes, my mom wound up tighter every day. Arrangements still had to be made, the sets weren't finished, the actors stubbornly refused to say their lines with the right inflections, and Mom questioned why she ever took on this project in the first place. My dad would take responsibility for something—anything—and she would let him. But that didn't stop her stress from rising to volcanic levels with the deepest blame of all: If Xanda were here, everything would be different.

It was like this every December in the weeks approaching Christmas as the three of us prepared for the most important night of the year—the same night, five years ago, that Xanda had disappeared. Every year I wondered how our memories of that night could so easily be eclipsed by a church Christmas play. But every year it happened again.

Lexi could no longer be eclipsed—either by baggy clothes or by my family's deliberate silence on the subject. I knew better than to complain about the back pain, the insatiable hunger, the tossing and turning, a body increasingly out of my control. I also knew better than to share the secret joys. The feeling of a small foot tracing the contour of my side. The bizarre, sequential jolts that I suddenly realized were hiccups. Wondering, as I searched the blacks and whites of her ultrasound picture, if her mouth would be like mine, if her eyes would be like Kamran's. If some piece of Xanda's soul could be wrapped in her flesh. These things were mine alone.

If anything was looking up, it was my job at First Washington Credit Union. I guess Shelley felt like she couldn't be such a tyrant after I'd met DaShawn and could blackmail James with Turkey Talk.

When I was in the break room sketching my picture of Lexi, she came up and looked over my shoulder. "Is that your baby?" She peered at the ultrasound print as I had first done, puzzled and with a trace of awe.

"Yeah. I mean, that's what her bones and stuff look like."

"Her? You know it's a girl?" I nodded. She pulled out the chair next to me then paused, like she wasn't quite sure if she could invade my space. There was still the weirdness there, turkey or not.

"Is that her face?"

I nodded. "You can't really tell, though, what she's going to look like. But you can kind of see where her nose is, and her forehead. And that black hole there? That's her stomach." It felt strange to be explaining this, this map of Lexi.

"How many weeks is she?"

"Well, this was a couple of months ago, when she was eighteen weeks. She's almost twenty-four now."

"Twenty-four," she echoed.

"How come you and James don't have a kid?" I asked.

"We do." One of the tellers swished past and poked me on the arm, probably wanting me to cover so she could go out for a latte.

"Well of course, DaShawn is your kid . . . but I mean . . . don't you want to have your own?" There was more to this story. Maybe James didn't want any more, or they thought it would be bad for DaShawn, or worse, they couldn't.

The pause stretched out. "Yes, I would love to have my own."

"Hey, Rand," the teller interjected, "do you think you could come help me find a couple of files?" She was giving me the *Shut up, I'm saving your ass* look, the one I had seen on Xanda's face a million times. I looked at Shelley for anger, but all I saw was sadness.

"Are you some kind of an idiot?" the teller hissed when we got to the filing wall. "Or do you just have a death wish?" The other teller, at the counter with a customer, peeked over her shoulder.

"What did I say?"

"You mean you don't know? Oh, you're not *that* stupid, then."

"Know what?"

"Shelley had a miscarriage a month ago—I guess that was before you came. But I'm not about to let you set her off . . ."

But I was no longer listening. I was thinking of Nik and Micah James. It was so easy. You're pregnant, then you're not. What would I do if I lost Lexi, too?

"Oh, my God," I gulped. "I'm sorry." Lexi shifted, my popped-out belly a reminder that I had what Shelley wanted. Deep down she probably thought I didn't deserve it. Suddenly her behavior—questions, suspicion, disapproval—all made sense.

The teller waved her hand impatiently. "You'd better watch yourself next time."

The thought of losing Lexi wouldn't leave my mind as she danced all afternoon in a postlunch sugar high. She had gone from the size of a tennis ball to the size of a soda-pop can in a little over a month, taking me to a new and uncharted level of exhaustion. It was even more tiring to keep avoiding Shelley when the space we all worked in wasn't much bigger than a hospital room. After throwing myself into shredding and filing for an hour, I was falling asleep in my peppermint tea.

The next time Shelley lumbered past, I said her name and she stopped. "Can I talk with you?"

She turned around, leveling me with her gaze. "Do you want to come into my office?"

It came out all in a tripped-up rush, not the steady, matter-of-fact question I'd rehearsed in my head. "That's okay, I just wanted to ask if I could leave early today."

And even though she nodded, I had the feeling anything I said would be wrong.

My thoughts were reeling as I drove away from First Washington Credit Union. Practically everyone I knew had had a miscarriage. Shelley lost a baby. Nik lost a baby—two, even. Micah James and another, earlier one.

Faith manages, they'd both said . . .

I nearly rear-ended the car in front of me.

It didn't seem possible coming face-to-face with her, with Shelley. No, with Nik. Even though I knew she lived in the Northwest, the coincidence was just too unbelievable.

I tried to reconcile what I knew of Nik with what I knew of Shelley, who had seemed to hate me from day one. A miscarriage . . . that was something else entirely. If she had been pregnant—someone who had wanted a baby for so long; if she had lost it and had to keep coming to work as if nothing had happened; if she had been forced to hire me, someone who had a baby coming but shouldn't. . . .

It all made sense.

Things happen for reasons we don't know, Nik would say, and I could hear Shelley saying the words, too. But she didn't know the married college student online was a seventeen-year-old high-school student in real life. I couldn't imagine what snippet of wisdom she might come up with for that. Being discovered would be like peeling back one more layer in my quest to be like Xanda: the rebel, the sinner, and now the liar.

Then there was Lexi. It was still possible to leave all of this behind with her and just . . . escape. I had money saved from my job at the bank, and there was still my portfolio. There was Boston. There was L.A. There was . . . somewhere.

Street after street whizzed past the car and my unfocused eyes. A silver Prius nearly sideswiped me, honking its shrill, eco-snobby horn.

"I couldn't even see you in the rain, moron," I murmured to myself, just now looking up to see that I was crossing Broadway, now 12th, now 24th.

Unconsciously, I was driving home, where my mom would be the last person I wanted to see.

I took a left on Madison to the only warm, dry place I could think of to be alone. The church would be empty, the staff gone, and the montage troupe not due for another hour and a half. The stained glass would be lit by the twilight, where the fragments of color formed a kind of hidden picture.

If I searched long enough, I might even find Xanda there.

Twenty-seven

A few minutes later, I pulled into the church parking lot, empty except for a cluster of construction trucks and my dad's Ranger.

It seemed forbidden, running into Dad without my mom watching over us, as if he were somehow to blame for this present disaster. I parked the car.

I heard Dad before I saw him. The hundred-year-old doors led into a brick building as dry and freezing on the inside as it was wet and freezing on the outside. Dad's laughter drifted into the foyer. I didn't realize it was him laughing until I peeked into the sanctuary. Dad was onstage with two guys I'd never seen before—young construction guys, definitely not from church. I knew this because just as I slipped into the back row, a set wall fell backward and one of the guys belted out a Xanda-style expletive.

Dad laughed. Mom would be horrified. I was fascinated.

This was a Dad I hadn't seen since Xanda died. The one who (a) relaxed, (b) laughed, and (c) laughed when someone else found a new and creative expression of the F-bomb. I half expected Andre to turn a corner.

One of the guys went around to the other side of the fallen wall and helped heave it upright while another bolted it in place. The rolling base my dad had designed would transform the stage from living room to battlefield in seconds, a skill he may very well have picked up at home.

Then a girl stepped out of the wings, wearing a tool belt, paint-splattered jeans, and boots exactly like the guys'. She couldn't have been more than twenty-two, the same age my sister would be, and was hauling a spool of electrical wire across the stage. My dad smiled and patted her on the shoulder like he'd never done to me.

In the darkness of the last pew, I sat for what must have been an hour, watching them build the sets, joking about clients and current events, totally unaware of me. I was transfixed by the Dad I remembered from my childhood. Watching him onstage with this girl was like watching what my life could have been like, if I could trace back far enough and start over.

She picked up baby Jesus from the manger and tossed him to Dad like a football. He held the baby for a moment before setting him back carefully and wagging his finger in mock warning: "Don't mess with Jesus."

I watched him while the sun sank behind the stained glass, until they started packing up to leave. I realized I would have to flee before he saw the car parked outside. And before Mom showed up.

Dad must have had the same thought, because he visibly transformed from this new, secret personality back to the Dad I knew, melting layer by layer before Mom could melt him herself. His shoulders slumped. He seemed distracted as the crew packed up, checking his watch and looking every few seconds toward the back door. The crew headed for the rear exit, slapping Dad on the back while one of them said, "See you in a few." Dad smiled casually but looked around once the last of his workers slipped out—and directly at me, though I was still masked by the glare of the stage lights. He looked defeated, utterly broken.

Sneaking didn't generally fall into a pregnant girl's skill set, but I managed it—no ordinary feat, considering the creaky, century-old floorboards and doors swinging with the weight of a hundred years. That is, until my heel clipped the edge of the door, the clunk of wood on wood echoing in the dark empty space with the hollow finality of a gavel.

Dad spun around and peered into the darkness, his lips pressing into a thin line. "Who's there?"

"It's just me, Dad." It felt strange to be alone with him, inside these hallowed walls and windows.

I gave him a wave and turned to go.

"Wait, Rand?" Dad called, crossing part of the distance. "Is your mom with you?"

"No," I said, looking over my shoulder to the darkened foyer. "I left work early and came here. Mom will probably come soon to start setting up for the rehearsal."

Dad was still walking toward me, slowly, as if I were some strange, unpredictable animal. I certainly felt like one these days, with new things happening to my body every day.

"How is . . . how are you? How is the baby?" he asked, still moving toward me in the most careful manner.

"Fine," I said, instinctively putting my hand across my front. "Kicking right now."

"Wow, kicking. I remember when your mother was pregnant with Xa—" He stopped, redirected, like he had hit the invisible wall. "When she was pregnant with you. You used to kick a lot, especially at night. Is it a . . . do you know what it is? I mean, have you thought of a name? I'm sure your mom . . ."

"Wait a second," I interrupted. *No one told him?* Of course he didn't know. I hadn't told anyone but Nik.

He shrugged, bumping up against the nearest pew. Then he chuckled, like it was no big deal. "No one tells me anything about these things."

"I haven't told anyone."

I closed the gap more, rifling through my sketchbook in search of the ultrasound picture. The shapes and shadows bending around Lexi would give us a tiny window into her dark, soft, safe existence. "Well, I have a picture somewhere . . ." I thumbed through the pages.

In seconds, the gap between us completely closed. Strange, but he seemed a lot taller close up—as tall as he had seemed when I was a little girl. He smelled like sawdust and wood glue from the set building, with a hint of soap. His skin looked older, drier than I remembered from those little-girl days. He watched me the same way I watched him—like he hadn't seen me for years, and he was taking all of me in for the first time. I was taller, too. My face more long, less round. The pregnancy. My hands stumbled with the strangeness of his sudden interest.

I fumbled through the sketchbook, turning page after page of drawings. I watched his face for a sign of recognition—that he would understand the secrets poured out of my heart and onto the page. But I saw only awe as he drank in the lines of my drawings like he was drinking in pieces of my life.

I passed a portrait of Xanda, and his hand darted out to stop me. The picture I stole from Dylan slid out of its place. His gaze stayed on the page for a moment more. "Where did you get that?"

"Someone who knew her," I mumbled.

Then he let go, and I flipped ahead and found the ultrasound picture taped in place. The first thing out of his mouth was, "Wow." It lingered in the air with hushed reverence. "Wow," he said again.

"Yeah." I was smiling in spite of myself. No one but me had a clue about how amazing she really was. And even more secret, what a gift she was from Xanda. "That's Lexi."

For a second, his face went white. "Lexi? Her name is Lexi? Like, Alexandra?"

"Yes."

The name hung between us, sucking the air out of our lungs. My dad reached out a finger to trace the contours of her face, the lightness of her bones. His touch was as soft as smoke. "What do you think?"

He reached her heart and drew around the four chambers. "I think she's beautiful." He put his hand on my shoulder. His skin snagged my red fuzzy sweater, the one I'd found in Xanda's things. The icy air cracked open between us, and all of a sudden it seemed like he was rushing to fill it. Especially when his eyes started getting red and his voice caught as he took a deep breath and said, "Miranda, I'm really sorry about all of this happening."

I wasn't sure I was ready for this. Having Dad's hand on my shoulder, on Xanda's sweater, asking about Lexi, was almost too much.

We both jumped when the sound echoed through the sanctuary. It was my mother's voice, saying, "Oh. My goodness."

Because she reserved God for the really important things.

Twenty-eight

"*What*," my mom hissed, "is going on here?" She looked over her shoulder—always looking to see who might be watching the family sins. I slammed my sketchbook shut.

We both started to answer her simultaneously. Guilty, though I couldn't even pinpoint what we were guilty of.

Talking. Connecting. Speaking the dreaded name of our family's worst blasphemy. Xanda or Lexi: it didn't matter which.

"Hill—," began my dad.

"Don't 'Hill' me. You know exactly what this is about, *Chuck*."

She only called him Chuck when she was really ticked, to remind him of the vast chasm between them. Chuck was a trailer-park name, she joked when she was in a better mood. She definitely wasn't joking now.

"I saw those . . . those *workers* driving out of here," she said, as if she couldn't even find a name for the scum of the earth Dad employed. "That *girl*. Did you have them working here, at the church? Around our daughter?"

My dad listened in silence. A stone wall, expressionless.

"And *you*," my mom said, turning to me, "how long have you been here? I thought you were working. Don't tell me you're skipping work now, too."

"I—"

Her face had tightened. Eyes narrowed. Teeth clenched. The same expression I remembered from the night Xanda died. "Chuck, did you have those guys around her? Is that what's been going on behind my back? Have you been letting her hang around with those *men*?"

"Mom," I started, "I was not hanging around—"

"You stay out of it." She looked down at my belly, which suddenly felt naked and stretched beyond capacity. "This has nothing to do with you."

It had everything to do with me and the vortex Xanda had left behind.

Lexi lurched, enough to make me stagger and reach for the back of a pew. Dad winced. I remembered the sound of Lexi's heart beating on the Doppler, my own beat thundering in the background with a heavy thud. Now my blood was racing around her at what must be a frightening pace.

"It has everything to do with her!" my dad suddenly roared. It stopped my mom in her tracks, loud enough to echo in the sanctuary like a lion let loose from a cage.

"Don't raise your voice in this building," said my mother with a look of disgust, as if his words were not even worth a response.

It must have been the aftereffects of hanging out with his construction buddies, cutting loose with whatever came into his head. Or maybe it was seeing Lexi's picture, knowing of her shape and her name, seeing Xanda's sweater on me, and being in a sacred place that gave Dad some mystical sense of strength. Otherwise, I couldn't explain why, after all of these years of shouldering the blame for Xanda's death, he would transform from a distant figure to a wall of defiance in one singular moment. Whatever it was, it froze all of us in place, as if God had come down from the heavens and smacked us upside the head.

"I said, *leave her alone.*" In one powerful movement, he filled the space between Mom and me, making both of us step back from the field of energy suddenly, terrifyingly surrounding him.

My mom opened her mouth, but nothing came out. We all stood there suspended, waiting for him to say more, or for something else to snap. For a window to crack open, or maybe for the gates of hell to swing wide.

When nothing came, Mom laughed nervously, pushing past him as she swept toward the stage. "People will be showing up soon, Charles. You'd better get the rest of these tools cleaned up."

I was still petrified, standing behind my dad as his shape transformed from the enormous wall of power back to the crumbling wall of shame. All that was left of his rebellion were two clenched fists.

But I was in shock. In shock that my dad—my own, invisible dad—had stood up for me, however briefly. I was floating up, up, up, past the glass and into the dark sky, like the white bird in my drawing. The part of me still in the church could hear Dad snatching his tools and disappearing out the back door while Mom looked over her script for the one thousandth time.

"Mandy!" My mom snapped. "Are you listening to me?"

"What?" I whispered, returning to my body with a shiver.

"Collate these new pages for me while I get things ready onstage." When I hesitated, she barked, "Get moving! People are going to be here any minute and it would be nice to have some help here."

That's right. I had to bring myself down to earth before the saints came marching in. We were all saints or sinners in my mother's mind. I'd swapped titles in one swift meeting of sperm and egg.

But what about my mom? *They've been lying to you all along,* Dylan had said.

If pregnant girls were sinners, what were liars called?

Twenty-nine

Montage opening night was sure to be a packed house for Essence Hannah, breakout actress. Mom couldn't stop telling everyone about her *Guys and Dolls* part or the Cornish application, or how they would be blown away by her performance. I would be backstage looking out over the crowd, trying for one more year not to think about the night Xanda died.

While everyone else headed to the Winter Ball, I waited on the couch in the First Washington lobby for my mother to pick me up. She would be rehearsing lines in her head for last-minute changes. I was rehearsing lines as well—the conversation I'd had earlier with Kamran replayed in my mind over and over.

I was late to English class that morning with stomach

cramps. Just before I reached the door, Kamran came out with a pass. We nearly crashed into each other.

"Miranda," he said, "it's you." Like we hadn't crossed paths nearly every day since last summer. Like he hadn't been avoiding me all along.

"We should talk," I said. "Before . . . well, before . . ." I touched my belly. Even at almost twenty-six weeks, it looked ready to burst. I couldn't imagine what I would look like at forty.

The key paddle dangled in his hand, jingling. His hair was longer than last summer, grown out over the collar of his jacket. "I'm not sure what there is to talk about."

Our English teacher's voice droned faintly through the door. I just stood there with his eyes drilling into me. "Well, even if you don't care about me, I thought you would be a little more interested in the baby."

He laughed, the same sound I had heard a thousand times, only never this harsh.

"I don't know what's funny about that," I said.

The laugh ended abruptly. "It's funny because I'm not so sure that it's mine."

What?

"I'm not so sure I'm the only possible candidate here. Because I've been finding out there's a lot more to last year than I thought. Delaney—"

"Delaney?" I cried out, then lowered my voice. "What has Delaney been telling you?"

Kamran ran his hands through his hair, a gesture I remembered like it was my own. "I always knew there were things you wouldn't tell me, but I was trying to give you space—I thought it was about your sister. But all the time I was studying and working, you were going out—parties, camping trips . . . always keeping things from me. What else am I supposed to think?"

"If you would just give me a chance . . ." *I would tell you there has never been anyone but you.*

"I did give you a chance. I thought you were different, Miranda. I've gotta go."

I came to work with my mind reeling. I could talk to Nik. Could I talk to Shelley? For a week now, I'd been baiting her with things like, "I saw *Femme Nikita* last night. Awesome movie."

"Mmm-hmmm."

Or, "Hey, Shelley . . . what do you think of the name Nicole? Nik, for short?" She only frowned. I didn't dare mention reading baby websites or ask if she'd had more than one miscarriage. If I was wrong, I would only be reminding her yet again.

Finally, she asked, "Is there something you want to talk to me about, Rand?"

After that, I stuck to filing and shredding and generally trying to stay out of her way.

Looking at the clock a million times didn't make my mom appear any quicker, so I headed to the break room for hot water and lemon. My belly didn't make it easy to push out of the soft cushions and into an upright position without flashing the lobby. As I turned to reach down for my sketchbook and satchel, I heard a voice behind me. Or rather, more like a low whistle of appreciation.

For me?

"Nice legs," said the voice: male, sultry, with a hint of an accent. Familiar, in a distant kind of way. I wasn't agile enough anymore to flee, but then I wasn't sure I wanted to. In any case, I couldn't stand there showing my backside forever. Who knew what hottie or creep could be standing there.

I did turn. More like arched, curiosity getting the better of me.

I knew him.

Andre.

In the split second we locked eyes, I saw how his face was older, more worn, but still the same boy Dad brought into our house so long ago. Almost six years, and I remembered every detail.

He squinted. "Don't I know you?"

"Excuse me," I pled, but he caught my arm. The smell of him floated past me, the same smell I remembered. Musky and sour and spicy, the smell that permeated Xanda's hair and now almost brought me to tears.

Before Dylan's Halloween party, the last time I saw Andre was my twelfth Christmas Eve. I fell asleep the night before to the merry tones of Xanda and Mom screaming about abandoning the family for "that boy." It was exciting—Xanda defying our parents to be with him. Mom made her promise to come home for Christmas Eve dinner, and we would all go to the closing night of the montage together.

That was the year Xanda refused to act in the play, when Mom cast me in my first and last lead role.

Xanda showed up for Christmas Eve dinner with Andre in tow, looking too cool to be uncomfortable. She wore a skirt so short I saw her panties when she spun to throw her arms around him.

It wasn't long before the shouting started. "Take that skirt off this instant and go put on something decent," ordered my mother. I couldn't wait to wear something so indecent myself. While my dad rolled his eyes at Andre, I was busy memorizing every detail of Xanda's revolt.

"This instant?" she countered.

"This instant," echoed Dad.

"Fine." And with one dramatic rip, the skirt was in Xanda's hand. The panties underneath exposed her two round cheeks. Andre smirked—I had the feeling he had seen this display before.

And that was when everything shattered. First, the skirt went into the fire and hissed with melting finality. Next, Mom grabbed the afghan off the couch and lunged for Xanda, who dodged and hid behind Andre. "Get out of my way," growled Mom. But Andre wouldn't budge. Xanda grinned from behind him. So Mom did something that shocked everyone—quick as lightning, she clutched Xanda by the hair and dragged her, whimpering, toward the door. Dad opened it on cue, and Mom pitched Xanda into the icy, holy night.

Then she turned to Andre. "Get *out*." He didn't argue, but as he left, he muttered something about my mother burning in eternal agony.

Once it was all over, Mom hugged me, crying, kissing my hair. "Never do that, Mandy," she whispered. "Never."

When I went up to my room to change clothes, I heard Xanda climb through the bathroom window and rifle through her things, the bars on her own window a mere inconvenience. A few minutes later, everything was silent.

But I saw them, below on the street. Andre looked up. Even from that distance, his eyes pierced me. I knew I might never see them again as I listened to the roar of his Impala fade into the valley.

In the end, my body didn't give me away. It was my eyes. He met my gaze, and he knew.

"I do know you. You're Xanda's little sister." He appraised my bump. "Well, you used to be little, anyway."

My arms instinctively wrapped around my belly. I could barely breathe under his scrutiny.

"Mandy! Mandy, that's right. Like Xanda but with Mmmm."

"Rand. I go by Rand now." For so long I had dreamed of this moment—flirting with the boy who loved my sister, who would have run away with her if not for her death. But never in my dreams did it go like this, under the fluorescent lights of the bank lobby, where my mom could storm in any second.

"Rand. Well, someone was randy with you, huh?"

"It's my—" My what? My ex-boyfriend's, the guy who was supposed to be like *him* except things didn't quite go as planned? "Never mind," I finished lamely.

"Didn't work out?"

"No. It didn't work out." It was the first time I admitted it out loud.

He reached into his pocket and pulled out a business card. *Andre Velasquez, Odd Jobs.* Under his name, a P.O. box and a cell number. I cradled it in my hand when an all-too-familiar version of my name sliced our conversation in half.

"Mandy?"

Mother. Here. To pick me up. And I could tell by the look on her face that she recognized him, too.

I stuffed the card in my pocket, the adrenaline I needed to escape Andre's orbit suddenly appearing in embarrassing abundance. I threw my coat around my shoulders and scurried toward my mom, who stood in the open doorway.

Shelley's eyes followed me. *One more reason for her to think I'm a train wreck.*

My mom said nothing, only aimed and fired a laser beam to unlock the car. I ducked in like she'd just read me my rights.

The car doors shut with a suffocating *thunk*.

Thirty

Mom drove with her eyes straight ahead, boring into the road. But I knew better.

It was dark already, almost the darkest night of the year. Our windshield wipers squeaked every half second, whipping back and forth as we drove to the church.

She said nothing. I tried to imagine what was going on in her head after what she'd seen. Me, talking to the boy who killed my sister.

Maybe I was wrong—maybe she hadn't recognized him. And if she had, maybe I could convince her *I* hadn't. Five years ago, I was just a kid. Twelve years old.

I guarded his card in my pocket like a precious pass to the future. A wild image flashed through my mind of driving to L.A.—a boy, a girl, and a green Impala. If he couldn't go there with her, maybe he would go with me. And when we got there, maybe he would tell me what really happened to my sister.

Meanwhile, next to me, the mountain of my mother simmered. "Did you think I wouldn't find out?"

I opened my mouth to respond, but the next onslaught filled my throat like sand.

"Have you been seeing him?"

A strange fluttering was happening in my lower back, tightening, as if by her voice, my mom was pulling on the connecting wires of my body.

"Because if you are, that's sick. He is sick. He's a grown man, and you are a little girl. Is that what you've been doing behind our backs?"

No, no I wasn't. I didn't.

"Are you even working at that bank?" My mom's voice had begun to rise. "What were you doing, talking to him? First you get pregnant, then you're sneaking out, then you're hanging out with your dad's crew, now you're seeing—were you planning to run away?"

"No—"

"Then what were you planning?" The shriek had reached metal-melting properties, the strings around me tightening, tightening.

"I wasn't planning anything."

"What was he doing there? Don't you remember wh*at he*

How you

Why were you

Why he

He

You . . . you . . . you . . . you . . .

Xanda . . . you . . . Xanda . . . you . . ."

The shriek wrapped around me in a high, desperate hum, settling into my body as a ball of blinding *pain, pain, pain,* purple and swirling hotly in my pelvis like mercury in my veins, creeping toward my heart, threatening to stop if she didn't stop screaming at me or if this pain didn't stop, screaming voice and screaming pain shouting *stop stop stop stop.*

"Stop." My voice slid underneath the din like blood seeping under a door. A fire engine screamed past with sirens blaring, but I could barely make it out from under the shrieking curtain of pain. My vision tunneled into blackness with Xanda's image at the other side, reaching out for my hands as I drifted, heavy with my small burden, reaching out to let Xanda take it off of my hands, silently offering me a way out. Or was she offering something else?

". . . and if you think I'm going to let you make the same mistakes, then . . ."

"STOP!"

The car and her screaming whirled to a stop, and I could dimly make out a red light at the top of my field of vision. The rain came down in dark, drizzling sheets.

"What, Rand?" And more silence, as loud as her shrieking had been.

You're killing her. I didn't realize I had whispered it until my mother responded with, "Killing who?" But I was already out in the street, painted by raindrops, water streaming down my hair and face as I slipped between the cars, across the road between a strip of businesses where she wouldn't be able to follow me in her luxurious, lumbering boat of a car.

I slipped in and out of darkness and water and pain, until the strings she had been tightening with her voice let loose and my body returned to normal, and by that time I was past the park and a secondhand record store and a café and a few brick apartment buildings, and the rain soaked my coat and the outside of my satchel. I didn't stop until I reached a covered corner near the bus stop, crowded with workers and students going home for the night and a homeless guy muttering and extending an empty hand.

My sketchbook and cell phone were still dry inside the satchel. My top five numbers were Home, Kamran, Delaney, Chloe, and Essence. I couldn't call any of those.

I had Nik's number stored from the BabyCenter days, though I'd never called her and couldn't imagine doing it now. What would I say? "Uh, hello, Nik, who might really be Shelley—this is XandasAngel, who is really Rand, who is really a pregnant teen and not a married art student. I just had a fight with my mom because of that guy you saw me with in the bank. Do you think you could come pick me up?"

That would go over like a miscarriage.

My belly lurched again, driving its tendrils of pain up and around the muscles holding Lexi, squeezing us both into a hard knot. Wrapping my arms around myself, I felt the paper in my pocket crinkle. Andre's card. *Andre Velasquez, Odd Jobs.* I wondered if picking up his stranded ex-girlfriend's sister from a street corner fell into that category.

He picked up on the first ring. "'Ello?"

I almost hung up.

"Who's this?" I could barely hear him past the rain and the homeless guy's shouting.

"It's me, Rand. Miranda. Xanda's little sister. Um, we were just at the bank, remember?"

"How could I forget?" Twelve-year-old me quivered, like the safety pins of Xanda's dress.

"I was wondering . . . do you think maybe you could pick me up?"

I couldn't figure out whether the silence on the other end was stunned or satisfied until a low hum swelled into a long *mm-hmmm.* "Yeah. Be right there." No questions asked. It might have been thrilling under other circumstances.

"Are you at home?"

"No. Actually, I'm at . . ." Where was I? The neon sign above my head blinked. "Cassandra's Salon Supply." I gave him the cross streets.

I didn't really know this neighborhood, which boded well for eluding my mom. We were definitely in the wrong part of town for her comfort level, but exactly in the right part of town for Andre's. By the time he drove up to the curb in his green Impala, the pain had subsided enough for me to waddle out there, forlorn and pathetic. I slid in, at once knocked out by the strong odor of cigarettes, grease, and beer. Morning sickness had been gone for months, but the scent of a forgotten hamburger in the backseat and a full ashtray were enough to push me to the edge.

Rain continued to come down, dampening whatever holiday spirit lit up this part of town—HAPPY HOLIDAYS blinked alternately with the time, 6:47 P.M.—and the temperature—46°F—on the light board across the street.

Opening night was in a little over an hour. I had that much time to get Andre to take me to the church and to play my part—the part of *that* kind of girl.

"You wanna go somewhere?" Andre looked at me expectantly, a crooked smile on his face.

"Yeah, I wanna go somewhere. Take me to where Xanda died." The smile dissolved into shock.

He stepped on the gas.

Thirty-one

The Impala had cleaned up nicely since the crash that killed my sister. If the inside smelled like ashes and dead meat, the outside looked brand-new. The windows were lighter than I remembered, when I peered out my bedroom window to see Andre's and Xanda's shapes moving in the shadows like dark fish in a murky pond.

All I could think about was the fact that I was sitting in Xanda's seat, soaking her into my body the way a flower soaks up sun and air. The echo of her life impressed itself into my very bones. The baby could feel it, too, I thought. It had to be why she kept pressing to come out.

The front seat was one big uni-seat—no console or stick shift or even a cup holder. Just seat, all the way across, with nothing to stop Andre from grabbing me and sliding me over to him if he wanted to, like he must have done with Xanda a thousand times. The pain came in another, shocking wave, as though it were channeling Xanda's spirit telling me *Stay away, stay away.*

And we could have turned around. I still had my cell phone. But for all I knew, he had taken Xanda all the way to Hollywood and she was waiting for me. Maybe he was taking me there now. I wanted to ask him, but his mouth looked like a prison door. Locked. Why hadn't he gone to prison, if what my parents said was true?

Andre started to light up a cigarette in the car, then gave my belly a bitter look and rolled his window down to toss it out.

"I said I wanted you to take me to where Xanda died," I said, hoping he could only hear the resolve in my voice and not the panic in its undercurrent. He picked up speed. Had he been drinking? I didn't want to get close enough now to find out, but I could smell something. Something that wasn't quite right. I wondered if Xanda had smelled the same thing before she plunged to her death.

Somewhere I remembered hearing that smell was the only sense connected directly to memory. The combination of wind and smoke and sweet sourness transported mine to the middle of the night long ago, to my bedroom window peeking out onto the street, close enough to the front porch to hear voices as they crept toward the house, kissing, rustling, sharing a cigarette. I peered from the darkness to see her hair dusted with moonlight, blue reflection on slick, black hair, slick, smacking lips, giggling and wafting in the sweet, sour smell that whispered secrets and freedom and sacred plans.

And then, I remembered, a different kind of smack broke through the whispers.

Smack. And, "What the hell was that for?" from Andre's lips.

I remembered the words because I knew how much trouble I would be in if the word *hell* ever crossed my lips the way it regularly crossed Xanda's. My mother would have smacked me the same way Xanda had just smacked Andre, with about as much mercy.

"You know what that was for." It was the voice she used when you didn't know what she was going to do—the one that made you hide in the closet and hope her wrath would pass as quickly as it came. I hid scars from that voice even from myself, swaddling them up and tossing them out the window like the cigarette Andre was tossing into the street now. The landscape screamed past us in his Impala.

My demand still hung in the air. *Take me to where Xanda died.*

"Yeah, yeah, I heard you," he said to me.

"So where are we going?"

His eyes narrowed. What once looked brooding and sexy looked almost menacing now. "You Mathison girls are all the same. Trying to trip everyone up with accusations and . . .

whatever. I told her. I told her, and she couldn't handle it."

And then I remembered what had happened while I spied on them from my window.

She had slapped him. Hard. And he said, "What the hell was that for?" And she said, "You know what that was for. That was for you and *her*."

"What *her*?" he mocked, exaggerating the word in a high, breathy imitation of my sister's throaty voice. I remembered feeling angry, because I imitated her voice, too. Practiced her laugh, still had it to this day, the kind of laugh you get when you've just gotten over laryngitis. It sounded hateful, coming from him at that moment, and then my sister said, "The *her* I smell all over you. The *her* that's in your pocket." A crackle. The sound of someone backpedaling for his life. And me, feeling excited and angry and terribly clever for being at the right place at the right time and inserting myself so seamlessly into Xanda's secret universe. Every nerve in my body on fire, ready to flee in case of detection and avoid certain death.

"What, you mean *her*?" Andre's voice had changed into something else, something resembling my own voice, or my father's—soothing, pacifying, lulling my sister with its apologetic tones. "You're crazy. She's no one." We all balanced on the edge of this knife blade. Was it truth? Was it fiction? What would my crazy, spectacular sister do next?

Nothing. Or at least that's how it sounded to me. Only shuffling, rustling, smacking, but the soft smack of kisses, like the hugs she would give me after one of her explosions. I could barely remember those explosions now. I wondered if Andre still did. I stayed a long time under the window, balancing on that knife and hoping for something more until I was too sleepy to balance any longer and crept back to bed and dreamed of sweeter things, like Christmas. And the safety-pin necklace I made to go with her dress. I knew she would love it.

Andre's Impala slowed as we approached a long stretch of road leading down to the airport, streams of cars on the highway lighting up the night.

We veered toward the embankment. It seemed tragically ordinary, that slice of pavement littered with butts and weeds and sparkling glass dust.

He stopped the car and wouldn't look in my direction. Instead, he watched the traffic snaking beneath us under the bridge just ahead.

"Here we are. Where Xanda died."

The sound of her name in his mouth was like an explosion in my mind.

For so long I had thought about this moment, the secrets of Xanda's life and death flayed open for my inspection. For five years, my parents had been stitching the secret back in place, but here it was. Open. Bleeding.

"So, do you want to get out of the car?" Andre was looking at me. I could feel his eyes on my face as I avoided his gaze.

"Not yet," I said, staring at the place he had pointed to:

a bleak span of concrete streaked with long black scrapes, a collage of metal and rubber left by decades of unsteady drivers. I imagined the moment the Impala struck the rail—the smashed windshield, her blood seeping into the foam and seams. I wondered which scrape was Xanda's.

We sat together in the silence, time passing like the stream of cars whizzing beneath us on the highway. Another wave of pain threatened to engulf me, and I isolated it in my mind. It began the size of a marble and swelled into a watermelon, pink and fleshy and throbbing. Giving in would mean going back, something I wasn't ready to do yet. Not until I knew everything. Not until he told me the truth.

"I'm ready," I said, reaching for the Impala handle.

A cloud of city sounds enveloped us outside the car. Maybe Andre would take me to Hollywood if I asked him to. I could do animation, painting backgrounds. Or paint scenery, or draw storyboards for big-name directors. If I had a tenth of Xanda's courage, I could do any of those things, taking her place at Andre's side. I could pick up where she left off, except with Lexi, too.

But looking at the concrete sobered me up. I half expected to see a pool of blood where she must have flown through the window, or maybe the safety-pin necklace still dangling off a reflector.

As we stood there together, looking at the spot of not-blood, not-Xanda, Andre reached over and took my hand. Suddenly I felt like the twelve-year-old again with the crush on my big sister's boyfriend who was nice to me long before any other boy was.

"My parents told me you killed her." Even as I said it, I could see this was an old wound for him, too. "I want you to tell me the truth."

Thirty-two

"It was Christmas Eve, remember?" It seemed absurd, standing by the side of the road and speaking of the living and the dead. The rain stopped, leaving rivulets of water threading through the gravel and glass like veins.

"Yeah, I remember. I could start with the fact that I hate your f—" He stopped himself, looking down at my belly. "Excuse me," he muttered. "I hate your parents." Then he was silent, and the traffic noise rose up between us again. He rummaged through his pocket and found his pack of cigarettes, lighting one up after moving downwind.

"Are you sure you don't want to go somewhere? Denny's or something?" He gestured toward his car—at once an object of his allure and the instrument of my sister's death.

"Not Denny's," I replied, disgusted. "I don't want to be hearing about Xanda at Denny's." A long, loud honking pierced the air and faded as it trailed down the highway—someone even more impatient than me. I felt myself resenting Andre for taking Xanda here to die. I wanted it to be a sacred place. Xanda deserved that, at least.

"I'm starving," he said. "D'you mind if we find a drive-through or something?"

I was about to shout, *Do you think I asked you to bring me here so that you could go get a burger?* when a cramp gripped me again and all I could muster was a weak "No."

A group of girls I recognized from school drove past in a beat-up Toyota—dressed in tight tops and tighter curls, wearing fur-lined jackets exactly like the one I had tossed into the donation pile last year. They were laughing together, even the one that had a belly like mine—the only thing I had in common with any of them. I turned away from the road, hoping they wouldn't recognize me. But they were too busy looking at Andre to notice me.

The memory of Andre and Xanda's fight slapped me back into the present, just like I wanted to slap his attention back from the girls to me. "Where were you going that night? Were you running away? Were you going to Hollywood?" I demanded. *Tell me a secret, and I'll tell you one.*

"I wasn't running away, that was all Xanda. I didn't have anything to run from. Not like her. She had . . . well, I guess you would understand."

"Running from my parents?"

Andre shrugged, taking another drag and blowing the smoke into the street. "Uh-huh. But not all of it. It wasn't all about running away. Some of it was running *to* something. Your parents didn't get it. Or they didn't want to. Xanda used to say she and I were so much like your parents that they should understand."

"What do you mean, like my parents?"

"You know—rich girl and the construction guy." *Chuck is a trailer-park name,* I could hear my mom laugh. My dad, who had worked his way from an apprenticeship all the way up to being a well-respected contractor, was still just *Chuck* in my mom's mind.

"But you and Xanda . . . ," I prompted.

Andre's brow furrowed in frustration. "She wanted . . . she wanted more than I could give. I mean, I was all up for going to Hollywood and everything, but she wanted . . ."

"More?" I asked. And suddenly, I could understand wanting more. Like my mom wanting more from my dad. Like I did with Kamran.

Andre continued, "Yeah. I mean, don't get me wrong, I loved your sister. She was just so . . . insistent. You know?"

Yes, I knew. It was one of her most prominent qualities. "But then what happened that night, after you left our house?"

Andre blew the last of the smoke from his lips and tossed the butt into a puddle, where it hissed and went out. I used to imagine what it would be like for those lips to touch my lips. The thought seemed completely foreign now. "You probably won't believe this," he said, "but I have asked myself that so many times, wishing I did something different. I mean, I warned her about . . ."

A pause. "About what?"

He wouldn't look at me.

"*Con leche*," I said, as much to myself as to him.

"She told you about that?" I could tell by the look on his face he was embarrassed. I had nailed something, even if I didn't quite know what it was.

"Yeah. I mean, no. Just that you were . . . well, she said you were a letch. Did you cheat on her?"

"No! That was the whole f—uh, the whole thing," he added, looking toward Lexi again. "I wouldn't cheat on her. I *looked*. I never, ever did anything more than looking." He slammed his fist on the hood, sending his cigarette pack flying and me jumping while he swore under his breath. "I swear to God, I didn't cheat. And it still wasn't enough for her."

He wouldn't look at me. Wouldn't look, even when I put my hand on his arm, like he was crying and didn't want me to see. It made him even more real to me. Not a *con* or a *leche*. Just a person whose well of loss ran as deep as mine. "I'm sure she knew you didn't," I said gently.

"All I had to do was *look* at someone, and your sister freaked out and accused me of cheating on her. Do you know why she died?"

He gave me no time to respond.

"Because she was pissed at me. Because we were headed to L.A. and we were on the road and I looked over at a woman driving next to me—and I didn't even *see* her looking at me, I swear, I was going to change lanes or something—and your sister flipped out. And I said I wasn't so sure we should be going to L.A. together, if she thought I was going to be screwing around on her all the time, and she started screaming at me more and threatening, and I said I was going to turn around, and . . . and you're probably not going to believe me, but after she threatened, she did it. She jumped from the car. *She jumped from the car.*"

And he kept on talking, yelling and crying and I was listening and crying and trying to imagine my sister putting the gun to her very own head, opening the door and jumping out of a moving car, with the pavement whooshing past, whooshing hard and fast and her throwing herself away from him, and being so angry and throwing herself out onto that hard, fast place—

"And your parents, they couldn't let the facts speak for themselves. They had to come after me, like I was some kind of criminal, and they wouldn't listen when I told them your sister jumped. No, they tried to tell the police I'd been drinking—I guess I had, a bit—but *we did not crash*, and I did not throw her out of my car like they tried to pin on me. They would not let it go. Your mother would not let it go. And she was going to kill me herself, for killing her daughter, her precious daughter, who when she was alive she called *hell on*

202

wheels. But all of a sudden when she was dead, she was Xanda the Angel, and I was the devil."

Xanda the Angel. Andre the Devil. I had lived with these archetypes for most of my life, twisting them into my own images.

But I couldn't make myself twist Xanda into the architect of her own death.

Because she loved life. She risked everything to live it. I couldn't imagine her choosing so flippantly to end it. "She couldn't have," I wanted to say.

But I knew she could. I knew, from the hole in the wall behind my door, when she threw a book at my head. I knew, from living with the fear that she might one day impale me with her stiletto, if she got mad enough. I knew, from the way she defended me to Mom, as if my life were more important than hers. I knew, even if I didn't want to know. And that was enough to break my heart.

Andre was still talking, as if his own personal dam had burst and was flooding me with all of his unspoken truths. "I was really sorry about your sister. I wanted to tell you, because I really liked you. You were a good kid. And your mother swore if I ever came anywhere near you, she would kill me herself. With your dad's nail gun."

I was crying, and Andre was crying, but we both laughed at the mental image of my mom wielding a nail gun, like she had ever wielded anything in her life more dangerous than a nail file. I did remember the police coming to our house. The reports. Being told to go to my room, and sneaking through the passageway to get closer, to catch snippets of conversation that would give me some clue as to why my sister died. I came away with one answer. Andre killed her. And somehow it was all my dad's fault.

Only it wasn't Andre. Somewhere in the branches of Xanda's life, something had taken a wrong turn, sending Xanda spiraling and then everyone else.

And then there was Lexi. How did she fit into these tangled strands? Could she still be Xanda's angel?

Andre turned toward me, his eyes rimmed with red and tears. "God, I still miss her sometimes," he said.

"Me, too."

"Sometimes, I think, maybe if I had done one thing different. Like if I didn't change lanes, or if I didn't look over . . . If I had been better about . . . I don't know. It's hard not to think about."

"I know." I took his hand—rough and dry, from building things up and tearing things down. Like my dad's, or a big brother's.

"It's strange to look at your face." He held my hand gently.

"Why?"

"Because it's like she is there, a part of you." He searched my face just like I did in the mirror—for signs of Xanda.

"Oh," he said, dropping my hand, "I forgot. There's something I have of hers that you might want. She had it with her when we left your parents' house."

Andre leaned into the passenger side of the car to dig through the glove compartment and came out with a chain dangling on his fingers.

The safety-pin necklace. The one I made, five years ago, and gave to her the night she died. I turned my face away, not wanting him to see what might lie there. My burning eyes fell on the place where she had jumped.

With my toe, I began to swipe away the gravel and glass, cigarette butts from a thousand drive-bys. And the more I cleared away the debris, the more I realized this should have been done a long time ago. Andre reached into the back of his car for a pile of fast-food napkins, and we set to work in silence, wiping away layers of grit and neglect.

I was wrong about Andre. About so many things. The Andre in my mind had been the one who would fly her away from our family bonds. The Andre before me couldn't even fly himself away from his own guilt.

In the back of the Impala, Andre had a hammer, nails, and a couple of white trim pieces. He fashioned them into a memorial and leaned it against the concrete with a few stones. I unlinked a few of the safety pins and encircled the wood, then put the rest of the necklace around my own neck.

But something was missing. Words. A picture. A name.

All I had with me was the photograph I stole from Dylan— and the pen-and-ink drawing of Xanda, the mazes in her hair leading to her face. Her eyes. The secrets hidden in her mind.

Here, with Andre, it seemed like I had reached the end, or at least the end of one mystery. Though some things about Xanda I would never know.

Together, we pinned my drawing to the cross.

Thirty-three

"You sure you don't want me to take you home?" Andre asked. His eyes penetrated the darkness, those eyes that had captivated the twelve-year-old me. I could see the kindness in them. We were both broken by the cross we shared.

"No," I sniffed. "I'm not going back there." Though technically, I supposed I could. The cracked dashboard clock said 8:39. Thirty-nine minutes past the premiere of the great Christmas montage, our house would be deserted. But after spending time with Andre, I knew where I had to go and what I had to do now.

He drove me to Elna Mead's auditorium, decorated in the Winter Ball theme—Always Remember This Night, chosen by Miss Delaney "Always remember how fabulous I was on this night" Pratt. A fluid arch of plum balloons blew in the crisp winter air, punctuated by the glow of silver-glittered stars dangling from the eaves.

As I watched Andre's Impala drive away, my last chance to flee drove away with him. The swell of pain crashed again, and I forced it back down. I wasn't sure I could stand this for fourteen more weeks.

Two teachers held the doors open, each giving me a quizzical look. But they smiled and grandly gestured me into the starry auditorium-*cum*-ballroom. A long line of couples snaked toward a plastic ivory tower gleaming against the plum background, white lights poking through like stars. Delaney and her minions had taken care of every last detail as if it were her wedding day. Black lights lit up tuxedo shirts, white dresses, and my maternity shirt in an eerie periwinkle glow.

Milo's voice boomed out over the PA system onstage, where he paced back and forth wearing a tuxedo jacket with shorts and a Freezepop T-shirt. "And here she is, the most magnificent planner and—if I do say so myself—a shoo-in for the currently open position of Queen of the Winter Ball . . . let's give a round of applause for the beautiful, the talented, the fabulous, the force to be reckoned with, Delaney Pratt!"

Delaney strode across the stage in a white column dress, poised with bashful humility. "Thanks, everyone," she said as the crowd hooted and clapped—everyone but me.

Kamran waited next to Chloe on the other end of the stage, and the gravity of what I had to do spread out before me. Tell him the truth. The whole truth. About Andre and Xanda. About Delaney. And most of all, about trying to make him into something he was not.

Milo broke into my thoughts with yet another enthusiastic announcement. "The voting will be revealed in a few short moments, folks. Don't go away, ladies and gentle-germs, we'll be right back atcha."

An affectionate groan rose up from the audience as Delaney descended the stairs. Her eyes surveyed the landscape and landed on one person, a girl who stood out in the crowd like a glow-in-the-dark barn. My chance to talk to Kamran alone had come and gone in a blip.

When she reached me, she dug her nails into my arm as she steered me out of the ballroom and down the stairs. Every step thudded with heaviness and finally ended in the auditorium basement, an expanse of concrete studded with pillars. Fluorescent tubes cast a pallid light onto Delaney's face. I forced the next wave of pain into a marble-sized ball.

"What are you doing here?" Upstairs, Milo once again reminded us from the podium that *the countdown has begun, ladies and gents.* "I know exactly what you're doing. You're trying to ruin this for me."

"I didn't come to talk to you. I came to talk to Kamran."

"He doesn't want to talk to you."

"Because of all the lies you told him about me?"

Delaney looked scornful. "I don't know what you're talking about."

The marble grew to a tennis ball. "Why did you tell him I was sleeping around?"

She didn't see Kamran follow us into the room a dozen feet behind her. How much had he heard already?

"Because he deserves to know the truth. Come on, Rand. I was at the same parties you were."

Those days flashed by in a blur. How we would show up together and end up apart—Delaney disappearing with Milo or someone else while I let her think I had done the same. It was what I wanted, to be like Xanda. Be *wanted*. To paint myself so successfully that Delaney—and now Kamran—couldn't tell the difference.

What had I done?

I shook my head. "But I didn't. You were going off with Milo or whoever, and I waited for you."

She looked confused. "You mean you never hooked up with any of those guys? How many guys have you been with?"

"Only Kamran." I glanced at him. His eyes were saying something, but I didn't know what.

"You're lying." Then she laughed. "That's so pathetic. Why would you do that? Why would you pretend?"

The pain rippled through me, and I thought, *This is it*. I was going to have my baby in the basement of the auditorium, and Delaney was going to be lecturing me the whole time. I couldn't wait for Kamran to chime in, asking me why, exactly, I couldn't be more like her.

"I wanted to be more like you. More like . . ."

"Xanda. Of course. It's always about Xanda. I'm so sick of hearing about your dead sister. More like Xanda. More like me. Why can't you just be real?"

"Okay," I said, too weary to argue. "Let's be real. Why did you get kicked out of View Ridge?"

Delaney went pale.

I don't worry too much if I only miss one, she had said.

It was as if she was no longer skin and makeup but a sliver of glass, hard and dazzling and clear—so clear I could see right through her.

"You were pregnant," I whispered.

Delaney said nothing, but her eyes told me the truth.

"And you came here to start over."

In that moment I saw that Xanda and Delaney were nothing alike at all, just as Kamran could never become the Andre of my memories. It wasn't fair to try to force him. Where Xanda felt bound, Delaney struggled to find something—anything—to tether her to the ground. Parties. Attention. And now Kamran—earthy, strong, and true. All this time, I thought Delaney had what I wanted. Now I saw it was just the opposite. She wanted what I had, and she took it.

Maybe Essence saw a piece of this when she tried to enlighten me. Enlightenment wasn't exactly right, but there was something religious about how I felt, peering through the worst pain I had ever experienced and for once in my life being entirely present, the moment wrapping around me like a cloak. Music echoed from the upstairs dance floor, punctuated by Kamran's steps as he walked up behind Delaney and didn't speak. My mother would call it an epiphany. Maybe Xanda would have called it a moment of perfection.

Milo's announcement boomed upstairs, a call to the Winter Ball royalty to take the stage. Delaney's face was wet, but I could no longer make out why. I was about to tell her to go back upstairs when the rush of sound in my ears enfolded me into a warm, dark cloud. Kamran stood behind her, sideways, and I wondered from the look on his face why he was still here—here, in this tunnel of darkness while Xanda smiled at me, a baby in her arms.

This must have been what Xanda wanted when she ran away with Andre. One luminous instant of perfect understanding and perfect peace, marred only by the icy concrete floating up to the side of my cheek.

Thirty-four

The darkness gathering around me and Xanda felt close, warm, like we were wrapped up together in our plaid sleeping bags when Dad took us on his annual camping trip. I don't know what happened to those sleeping bags after Xanda died. We never went camping again.

Being alone with her, in that warm, flannely memory, was like recapturing the Dad we lost, too. Except that we were in a tunnel, the darkness smeared by Xanda's faint glow and the glow of the bundle she held as she stayed several paces ahead.

As I followed her, groping and struggling to catch up, I passed darker places, places that looked like if I stepped into them they would swallow me up like one of Kamran's wormholes and deposit me into some other space and time.

Kamran's voice broke through one of the walls, like a claw reaching out to pull me in. Xanda and the baby slipped around a corner. I plunged into darkness.

"What is her name again?"

"Miranda. Miranda Mathison." Kamran's voice again. And someone else—Delaney?—saying, "Ohmygodohmygod ohmygod . . ."

A voice I didn't recognize said, "Hold her." Arms gripped me, light pierced me, pain enveloped me. Metal on metal, clanking. A woman with pale red hair hovered over me. Xanda was gone.

I couldn't breathe because of the cup over my mouth. I reached up to rip it off, sucking in air. Everything was so white, except for the two square, black eyes staring down at me from the wall, lights tearing through them at a furious angle. We were moving. But I couldn't move the cup off of my mouth.

"Miranda, listen to me," said the red-haired voice. "You have to relax. You have to keep the mask on. You have to breathe." She had no eyebrows. Or they were so pale they disappeared on her white, white face. "Do you understand me?"

There was so much pressure on my chest, pounding from deep inside my body. "Lexi." I didn't know if the words came out of my mouth or not because of the pounding in my ears. But the woman seemed to hear.

"The baby is going to be all right, Miranda. But you have to relax. If you don't relax, it's going to be very difficult. Very difficult for the baby." Her hot breath on my face was making my heart race faster. "Back," I said, or tried to say.

"I'm going to count, and I want you to breathe along with my counting. Can you do that for me? Raise a finger if you think you can do that for me." Instructions from my brain fired off toward my finger, but I wasn't sure if they got there. "Good," she breathed. "One . . ." Deep breath. "Two . . ." My heart was slowing down. "Three . . ." And I was starting to feel my body return to normal, the muscles wrapped around me finally releasing their cast-iron grip.

"Good," she said, and kept counting while I kept breathing, my heart rate slowing as I breathed, breathed, not daring to look at those two black eyes hovering in front of me or toward the voices—whether or not one of them would be Kamran or worse, Delaney.

My body felt warm and wet, like I was sleeping in a pool of sticky liquid. I tried to sit up and see what was happening. If Kamran was standing over me, I didn't want him to see me wet myself.

The redhead was watching a monitor, a green blip that seemed to be steadily going downhill. But her attention, for the moment, was away from me as I struggled to peek over the oxygen mask. We were alone in a small, white, moving room.

Then I saw the blood. A dark pool.

And I heard the cry.

The cry that was mine.

And the downward whine of the monitor as the sharp point pricked my skin and the liquid pool filled the room, up and over my head.

When I woke again, it was chaos around me.

The redhead and black-eyed windows were gone, and I could no longer feel the rumble of the road. Instead, I was in a cavernous hall with blinding lights overhead and the murmur of people walking every which way—coming in close for a look at my body, my shirt stripped upward and away from my stomach—now dotted with round, white monitors—and then rushing away, clipboards or instruments in hand. No one stopped moving. I no longer had an oxygen mask, but when I reached up to touch my face, I felt the pull of a tube inserted into the back of my hand. Clear liquid loomed over me in a bag dangling from a metal hanger.

Another frightening cramp gripped me, and I cried out, only this time it was my stomach, whose contents were threatening to spill onto the clean white sheet.

The threat became a quick, horrifying reality before I could do anything to stop it. Hot acid filled my mouth and nose while tears streamed down my face. If I hadn't been tangled up in tubes and wires, I would have lunged for the sheet to cover my humiliation. Instead, I threw up in front of a throng of scrubbed onlookers. But as another wave of nausea gripped me, I realized I didn't care. I only wanted it to stop. I was sobbing for it to stop. I buried my face in my arm until the

IV split open a crack and a tiny ribbon of blood branched out through the crevices in my skin.

"What is happening?" I cried, and a curvy, dark-haired nurse in scrubs rushed toward me with a towel.

"It's the magnesium sulfate," she muttered in my direction, giving the monitors a more critical eye than she gave me. "Some people don't react well."

A very great relief, I wanted to say, but I was feeling too nauseous to be a smartass. Instead, I zeroed in on the footsteps, the curious faces, the bright liquid stain.

"There's a boy in the waiting room who says he's the father. If he is, he can come—"

"No," I said. I couldn't forget the way he just stood there, watching. "I don't want to see anybody."

In a quick movement, she gathered the damp sheet and towel and whisked them off. My parts were all exposed except for a tiny towel the nurse tossed on her way out. Another towel was balled up, pink with blood.

"Wait," I called to her, and I realized I was crying. "What is happening to me? What is happening to Lexi?"

She stopped for a moment, her arms full and her face softening. "I'll try to send the doctor in soon. She can tell you what's happening. Just rest. We're doing everything we can to save it."

To save it. The words stuck in my head. But I couldn't speak, because the real me—not the me who was sitting half-naked in the ER attached to six monitors and a bag of magnesium *whatever*, but the me of my mind and heart—had floated away from my body like I was watching myself in one of my mother's plays, separated. On a stage, I would have screamed. First a whimper, then building into a wail, then a scream commanding every doctor in the building. To save her. To stop whatever they were doing and save her.

But this wasn't a play. No one was paying any attention to me, and I barely had the strength to move the towel to cover myself when someone wheeled in what looked like a very ancient ultrasound machine hooked to a monitor. I hardly noted his face, only the way he squirted the jelly onto my stomach in one quick, cold spurt and looked at the fuzzy image projected by the ultrasound wand. I had no voice to stop him when he rolled the machine away.

I had no strength at all to stop the new tears rolling down my face. I tried to sit up, to call to someone, when a spiral of dizziness captured me in its undertow. My eyes closed to keep the world from spinning apart.

Thirty-five

A pinch on my backside awakened me, pulling me out of the twists and tunnels of my mind. It was dark in the room, like a warm nightmare. I heard someone say, "Three twenty A.M. Another dose of beta metha . . . *whatever in twelve houuurrsss . . .*" And the room spun again, and I was back in a writhing meeting of time and space, drowning my lungs in liquid and parching my tongue with the most unbearable thirst.

"Water," I mumbled, wondering if some other tunnel was a flood while I had chosen the desert.

Kamran was here, and now he wasn't. Further down this shadowy passage was Lexi, a miniature copy of my sister, with accusation in her eyes. Her father—I'd sent him away. Would she hate me for it? But at least here she was still alive.

In another passage, translucent through the depths, her cold form lay wrapped in Xanda's arms.

As if through a thick layer of consciousness, I could feel my body tensing—slowly, murkily, in the way it had been since I last saw my mother. I could hear her voice echoing. *It's better this way.*

"I don't want you here," I said, and she vanished as quickly as she came. Then Nik appeared—or was it Shelley? They merged and divided, holding a tiny white bird.

The darkness parted, making way for a hazy light and voices.

Placental abruption, they whispered. *Twenty-six weeks. Too early. Magnesium sulfate, watch for lung fluid. Still having contractions. Blood.* The voices were underscored by a low, mechanical moaning and an insistent *blip blip blip.*

"Make it stop," I whispered, but the blip wore on. Another pinch, a poke, and darkness fell again. I lost track of space and time, though the terrible thirst hounded me through my dreams and nightmares. The floodwaters in my lungs and the waves of pain and the taste of acid refused to recede.

I knew I must be dreaming again. Because Xanda was there, holding Lexi in her arms and smiling like they were very old friends. Because the dark tunnels I had been traveling for so long were flooding with cold, fresh water, washing past our ankles and rushing into the hidden corners. Because I could almost breathe again. Because an angel who looked just like the ob-gyn hovered over me.

"Miranda," the angel's voice said gently, like the ob-gyn

would have done. She had long hair, bright blue eyes.

"Miranda, I'm here now. I came as soon as I heard you were admitted."

Admitted where? "To heaven?" I asked.

A strong odor hit my nose, smelling of metal and sulfur. Heaven smelled like the hospital. The ob-gyn angel laughed softly and stroked my cheek. "No, not yet."

My eyes blinked open, and it was true, though I didn't dare try to sit up. I was in a new place, a room with a wall of windows lighting up the ob-gyn's halo of hair. She stopped stroking my cheek and offered me a cup of ice chips. "Miranda, can you talk to me right now?"

I nodded, my mouth full of ice. I felt like I hadn't had a drink in days. "Your mother has been in the waiting room—"

"No," I said, too loud in my own ears. "No, I don't want her here."

"But—"

"No," I pleaded, my heartbeat getting louder on the monitor hovering over my head. "Please don't make me."

"We can't make you do anything, Rand," the ob-gyn said, patting my hand. "No one can come in without your permission."

I reached for my belly and felt Lexi's foot move underneath. Alive. Still alive. "What about Lexi?"

"She's okay, for now. But things are going to be difficult for both of you. Lexi needs you to be strong. Do you understand?"

I nodded my head, not really understanding anything. My

muscles began to clutch again. She gripped my hand as she watched the monitor needle arch upward, plateau, and then ebb. "We've been giving you a drug to try to stop your labor, but it's not working."

"It's making me sick."

"I know. But that part is over—it should be wearing off. You were having side effects—hallucinations and your lungs filling, which is why we couldn't give you any water. So our next step is getting the baby here safely."

"What is happening?"

"You are twenty-seven weeks pregnant right now, almost six months. Babies are supposed to be born at forty weeks, at the earliest thirty-six. But Lexi is different. She's trying very hard to come early, and we've been trying hard not to let her."

"Is she going to die?"

The ob-gyn took a breath. "The good news is, medicine has come a long way. It used to be that babies born at twenty-seven weeks had no chance, but now . . . it's better now. The bad news . . ."

I didn't know if I wanted to hear the bad news.

"Babies born very early can have problems," she continued. "Their lungs aren't developed, they are vulnerable to viruses . . . so many things. That's why we were trying to slow down your labor, to give her a few more days."

It was daylight outside, filtered by the cloud cover, and I couldn't tell how long I'd been there. A day? A week? The ob-gyn was wearing a wreath pin. Was it Christmas yet? How long had my mom been here?

"If she survives, she's going to be in the hospital for a long time. We're going to have to keep her in neonatal intensive care until she's strong enough to breathe and eat on her own. That's going to be a very long journey, with no promises."

She was still patting my hand, and the touch was starting to hurt. My skin hurt. My head hurt. My neck hurt, but I couldn't lift my head to make it stop.

A nurse came into the room and began to check my vitals. She nodded to the doctor.

"I need to check on another patient, but I will be back. The nurse will watch over you. Are you sure you don't want me to get your mother? Or do you have a sister who could come—"

"No."

"All right," she said. "But it would be good to have someone with you. The next twelve hours or so are going to be . . . difficult. You shouldn't have to face it alone. Here is your cell phone, just in case." Seven missed calls. "I'll see if I can track down the anesthesiologist for your epidural." She left me alone with the nurse.

No promises. At the same time I was seized with pain, I was also seized with a kind of feverish hope. She had said *if*. Like it was entirely possible Lexi would be born, and be okay. That she and I could still flee, like that white bird.

Still, it wasn't enough to hush the voices of fear splintering through my bones. What, I wondered, does faith do when it has nowhere else to go?

Faith manages, I could almost hear Nik saying in my head. She had a voice like Shelley's. One that could keep glass from shattering.

My cell phone still had three bars of juice, still on silent from being stuffed under the counter at work. I scrolled through my contact list until I found Nik's number, stored there since the BabyCenter days. Maybe it wasn't Shelley. Maybe she wouldn't hate me when she found out I'd been lying all along—no marriage, no art school. The only true thing was Lexi.

And Nik's baby. Micah James.

Help, I punched out carefully. *Baby dying. Need U. XandasAngel.*

Thirty-six

Once I hit SEND, it was too late to go back. No matter what, I would have some explaining to do.

She was probably sitting down for breakfast with her family. Maybe she had finally made it through a night without nightmares. Maybe today was the first day she woke up without crying. My message would be a jagged hook from the past.

So I couldn't believe it when, seconds later, my phone vibrated with a text message. FemmeNikita, reaching out for the hook I offered and grasping it like the hand of a friend. *Where r u?* Then, *I'm coming.*

I texted my location: *er uw hosp.*

The nurse checked my vitals—blood pressure high,

oxygen count low. She would need to hook me up to the oxygen again. "Your mom is out in the waiting room. Want me to show her in?"

"No." The baby's heartbeat was quick. Frightened.

A loud knock at the door sent my own heartbeat skyrocketing. Who would pound like that?

"Maybe that's her," she suggested cheerfully. "She's been out there for days."

The door started to open, and I panicked. "Don't!" I shouted. And before I could even see the face, I felt her judgment filling the space and suffocating me. Making me pay for the sin of missing Xanda too much.

A young man in gray scrubs appeared, bringing a gust of fresh air with him. He looked like Kamran, with the same olive skin, dark hair, and golden-green eyes, reminding me of how I had sent him away. I couldn't have him here, not when I knew what he thought of me. "I stopped by to see if she was ready for an epidural."

I reached out to the nurse and clutched her arm. "I don't want to see anyone."

"Not even your parents? You don't want family here with you?"

Xanda was a preemie. Was it her fault this was happening to me now?

"No. I don't want anyone here."

The anesthesiologist stood there awkwardly, looking back and forth between me and the nurse. "Um, maybe I should come back later?" The nurse held out her hand as if to say, *wait*.

"Maybe after an epidural you might want to have them with you. The contractions will be a lot easier then," she suggested.

"I don't want to see them! How many ways do I have to say it?" The oxygen monitor beeped impatiently.

The nurse's eyes widened like they might suddenly pop out of her head, then took on a look of deep sadness. "Oh, honey."

"I'm going to come back after I see my next patient," said the anesthesiologist, edging toward the door and silently slipping out.

The monitor next to my bed continued to draw mountains and valleys onto the ribbon of paper spitting out, tracking my contractions, minute by minute. Another one was coming. I had to relax. "Please don't let them come," I said with my last, deep breath.

She waited until I unfurled myself. "Well, let me know if you change your mind. Is there anything I can get for you? Some ice?"

I nodded my head. I couldn't speak. It was all I could do not to cry. A few minutes later she came back with a cup of ice chips, and I sucked them down fast.

"Oh," said the nurse, "and you have a visitor. *Not* your mom. At least, I think it's for you. Are you Xanda's Angel?"

I nodded.

"Yeah. There's a Nichelle Jones here to see you. Is she allowed into the fortress?"

"Nik?" I asked. The nurse nodded.

The only Jones I knew was Shelley.

Alexandra. Lexi. Xanda.

Miranda. Mandy. Rand.

Nichelle. Nik. Shelley.

I knew Nik. Nik knew me. And I knew I was fired for sure.

A moment later, the door opened slowly behind the curtain. And suddenly the room wasn't big enough for me and this enormous presence entering the room, this person who took one look at me and dropped the super-sized purse she was carrying, so that every pen, mint, and roll of quarters came tumbling into the room.

Her face transformed from surprise to reproach to pity in a matter of seconds. "Rand?" Her voice was soft and hoarse. "Rand? Is that you? You're Xanda's Angel?"

The weight of my lies gripped me in another contraction, one I was totally powerless to stop or even prepare for. The full force of it knocked me into a curled up, crumpled fold.

The spilled-out purse lay on the floor, totally unnoticed, while Shelley rushed to my side and wrapped her strong arms around me. "Breathe into it," she whispered. "Relax, and breathe into it. It's almost over. You're past the hardest part. Just a little bit longer."

I tightened up, almost wishing it wouldn't stop. I knew

when it was over, I was in terrible, terrible trouble.

"Nik?" I stammered.

She pulled away from me and took my face in her pink palms threaded with brown. She was going to hit me. Or hate me. Or tell me my job, my career, my life, was over.

But instead, she said, "Rand. It's okay." She stroked my cheek gently, so gently it felt like a whisper. "I'm here now. For Xanda's Angel."

Thirty-seven

"*I'msorryI'msorryI'msorry,*" I kept saying, as if chanting the words would not only pacify Shelley but would keep the fog of drugs and nausea and contractions away for a moment longer. My voice came out in a raspy crack.

Shelley held me tighter, stroking my hair. "Shhhh. It's okay."

"But you've got to understand," I panted, "I didn't mean to lie. I thought . . . because of Micah James." I winced and Shelley's eyes widened. "I'm sorry." If she wanted to leave right then I would have understood.

Instead, her face softened. "You remembered his name."

I thought of Xanda, whose name was right up there with the Lord's, taken in vain. It didn't occur to me no one would mention Micah James.

"It means he touched your life, for you to remember his name." Her eyes watched me with kindness I had never seen in my own mother's eyes.

"Will you stay with me?" I asked.

"Don't worry, I'm going to stay here. You're going to be okay. You're going to survive this."

Another contraction. They were somewhere around three minutes apart now. Shelley hugged me to her, her breath on my cheek.

"What about DaShawn? Is he okay? Is somebody taking care of him? You've got to have somebody taking care of him."

"Shhhh," she said, wiping my hair away from my forehead as if I were her little girl. Gently, her soft hands continuing to stroke my hair, so softly I wanted to cry. "He's okay. He's taken care of."

The wave crashed over me, worse than ever. *Thirty seconds. Twenty. Ten.* I could hold on for a few more seconds. Shelley's touch, comforting in the valleys, felt like fire on the mountains.

Four and a half hours later, I could understand why Jesus would say *It is finished*, after going through the worst pain of his life and coming out the other side. Outside the bank of windows, we could see the moon rising over the mountains.

Through the hardest parts Shelley had fed me ice chips, given me a pillow, taken it away, given it back and let me *scream, scream, scream,* wondering if my parents could hear me down the long hall and across the valley between us. I wanted them to hear me scream, the way they had never screamed for Xanda.

The pediatrician came into my room, conferring first with the nurses and then coming to my bedside to explain what would happen next. Orderlies wheeled in more equipment—a clear plastic baby bed on wheels with tubes growing out of it like snakes and gloves for reaching into it on one side. "This is the ventilator," the doctor explained, "for when the baby comes. She will need extra oxygen, and we'll need to take her straight to the NICU—the Neonatal Intensive Care Unit." She nodded her head several times, as if that would be enough to convince me.

I rested in the valleys between the mountains, even though they got shorter and shorter. The anesthesiologist never did come back, but the ob-gyn did, along with a crowd of medical people, checking to see my progress and Lexi's and then disappearing again until I screamed at Shelley, "What are they doing here, if Lexi's going to die?"

"Now you listen to me," Shelley said, staring hard into my eyes. "Nobody said this baby is going to die. You don't know that. Nobody knows that. They're doing everything they can."

I was breathing in short, hard puffs. "What about Micah James? Why would he die and Lexi live? It doesn't make sense!" I threw the pillow onto the floor again, knocking the rolling table and sending the cup of ice exploding across the linoleum.

"A lot of things don't make sense until down the road, after you've had some time. That's why we've got faith, baby girl." Her voice lowered to a whisper, or maybe I was caught up in the next whirlwind and couldn't hear. "Keep your eyes on the future, because that's where the answers are. It's where the hope is."

"That's not true," I heaved. "We make choices, and we pay for them." I couldn't lie down anymore. The pain in my back was killing me. I pulled myself to a sitting position on the edge of the bed, hooking my feet on the ledge below.

A mountain was pushing its way through my back so that I couldn't argue anymore. "Hold me!" I called to Shelley, and she pressed her full weight against me, pushing the mountain back.

The ob-gyn came in a heartbeat. I wondered for a split second if she was strong enough to catch the force sure to come out of me.

"Is it too late to stop the labor?" I demanded.

"Yes," the doctor said, smiling. "Way too late." I felt like slapping her for smiling. But I settled for grabbing my knees while Shelley held me, keeping me from coming apart at the seams. "Now slow down," she said, "and push when I tell you."

I stopped. And when she said to push, I did.

Then quite suddenly I was on the other side, barely

conscious, and here was this tiny, translucent thing like a wax-works doll, except she was purple and spindly and weighing not much more than a beanie animal, and looking more like a raisin than a human.

But beautiful still.

She had the shape of Kamran's head. Lips like mine. A heart-shaped face, like Xanda. Like in the ultrasound, except curves only hinted at in the shadows were rounded and pal-pable. And real. Absolutely, shockingly real.

"Time of birth: five forty-two P.M.," said the ob-gyn, and the nurse jotted it down.

"Five forty-two on Christmas Eve," said Shelley. "Your very own Christmas gift."

"Nothing good ever happens on Christmas," I panted. Still, I couldn't tear my eyes away from the baby. Wrinkled skin gathered around her joints with a layer of whitish flakes, protecting her from fluid and now from the world, which assaulted her with light, sound, air, and a roomful of people.

When she cried, she sounded like a new kitten. I could almost see her lungs through the tissue-thin skin.

They didn't even let me touch her before they put her into the little rolling ventilator and whisked her out of the room.

Thirty-eight

Shelley wiped her forehead as if pressing that mountain out of me was the hardest work she'd ever done. The nurse stayed.

"What's happening to my baby? Can I see her?"

"Soon. But you should rest now. They'll take care of her." She chattered on about how they had taken the baby to the NICU. Her lungs would be immature. She wouldn't yet have the sucking reflex. Her skin would be too sensitive to touch.

Shelley closed her eyes, "just for a few minutes," and before long her head had dropped down to her shoulder and she was snoring softly.

The nurse began to peel away the tapes and tubes and monitors sticking out of me like Dad gathering gift wrap to take out with the trash. It was like nothing had ever happened, except for feeling like I'd been hit by a truck. "Can I get you something? A Popsicle?"

"Just take this IV off of me," I said irritably, noticing where the skin had puffed pink at the edges of the tape. I picked at it with my left hand. When she rushed over to help, I softened. "Maybe you could get a pillow for my friend, too."

The room was quiet except for the low rumbling of Shelley's breathing. Even after the nurse left to tend to other patients, I couldn't rest. I felt empty. Anxious. I reached for my satchel. Ten missed calls. Kamran? My parents? I didn't bother to check.

I could put on my clothes and go home, and it would be like Lexi had never existed. Someone here—maybe Nichelle, who wanted a baby, *needed* a baby—would take her. My parents would have their daughter back. I could take back the part of Brenda, repent, and nothing at all would change.

Except everything had changed.

When I fell asleep, my phone continued to buzz in my dreams. The ground beneath me rumbled like a saw. I passed a white cross, a chain mail of safety pins. Xanda was nowhere to be found, even though I was sure she was with the baby—I could hear her voice speaking my name in a piercing whir.

Mandy.

The whirring sounded again—a phone ringing, somewhere in the room.

I sat up groggily. Shelley was gone, and in her place was a note scrawled in Sharpie—"Be back soon." A few streaks of golden light penetrated the sky from behind the mountains. What time was it? My phone buzzed in my satchel, tucked into the sheets beside me.

Seven thirty-five, Christmas morning.

Another ring assaulted my ears, dragging me fully into the present. Lexi. Where was she? I started to swing my legs over to the side of the bed then had to stop when a rush of blackness wrapped around my head like a turban. Slowly. I had to move slowly, or the parts still inside me were certain to fall out.

The phone rang again, nagging and insistent. "Shut up!" I shouted, and swung my pillow in its general direction, knocking the handset from the wall so it dangled helplessly in midair. A voice squawked on the other end like Charlie Brown's teacher. While I tried to regain my balance, it went dead.

Still swathed in a hospital gown, I pulled on the hospital drawstring pants and tried standing up. Dizziness went from the top of my head to my knees, threatening to buckle.

Slowly, slowly, slowly. But then another, more urgent voice, said, *quickly, quickly, quickly.* I made my way to the door, where a few medical papers with my name on them were tucked into a Plexiglas pocket. Past the door, down the long hall I limped to the center of a whirlwind of activity—doctors, nurses, wheelchairs, papers, patients, people bearing balloons and flowers, a desk in the midst of it all.

"Where's my baby?" I panted to the nurse at the desk, who dropped the papers she was thumbing through.

"Are you Mandy? I just sent a call back to your room. I think it was your mom."

"Where's my baby?" I repeated, with an undercurrent of *If you don't tell me, I'm going to peel your eyelids off.* "Is there somebody who can take me to see my baby?"

A tall, thin nurse with enormous eyes appeared and put her hand on my shoulder. I vaguely remembered her as part of the birth-room crowd. "I'll take care of this," she said to the desk nurse. "You shouldn't be up yet," she said to me. "Wait here, I'll be right back." In a flash, she came back with a wheelchair.

"She's in the NICU," the nurse said as she wheeled me toward a hidden elevator, pronouncing it "nik-you." The sound made me think of Nik. Shelley.

"Did my friend leave?"

"I don't think so. I think she went down to find something to eat while you were resting. I heard you had quite a night. And that you were very brave."

"I don't think so."

"You made it through birth. You should be proud of yourself. It's a unique, powerful experience." I couldn't see her face, but it sounded like she was smiling. "Of course, now you have the infinitely more challenging experience of parenting ahead of you." She pushed a button on the elevator before the doors swished shut.

If Lexi survives, I thought.

We emerged from the elevator onto the NICU floor. A

large picture window looked out over the rows of little incubators and ventilators, where babies hung on to the thread of life. A fat, hairless one wore a silver metallic jacket with light streaming out of the edges. A long and thin baby with a mop of black hair and purpley skin grew a network of cords out of its body, shaking.

I thought I would be able to recognize Lexi anywhere, a mirror of my own self. But I had only seen her for a split second, covered with white fuzz, before they'd whisked her away from me. Now, faced with twenty possibilities, I wasn't so sure.

But there she was, in the ventilator and cushioned by folds and folds of white blanket, a plastic tube taped to her nose and a diaper looking like it might swallow her whole. Skin so goldeny pink, like mine after a summer visiting my dad's parents in Arizona, brownish hair sprouting in a damp mass from the top of her head and feathering into wisps on her forehead. A lot of hair, like Kamran—the color a cross between mine and his. Sweet, tiny lips. Eyes closed. A circle of cord taped where her heart would be.

I was in awe.

"I'll check if you can see her."

"Is it okay? Or is she too . . ." I didn't know what. I only knew I was afraid to go anywhere near her, afraid she might shatter.

The nurse went to talk with the NICU staff while I watched through the glass.

A warm presence came up beside me, and I turned to see Shelley there, smelling like pancakes.

"Sorry I left while you were sleeping. I had to call my family and grab a bite."

"DaShawn!" I had forgotten all about him. "Oh my gosh, it's Christmas. You have to go home."

"I'll go soon. But I wanted to check in on you first. She's a beautiful baby. She has the look of you, I think. What's her name?"

"Lexi," I answered, like a magic spell threatening to break.

"It's a beautiful name. Does it mean something special?"

"It was my sister's name. Alexandra. Xanda."

"Xanda's Angel." A look of knowing passed over Shelley's face. "You must have been close."

I couldn't get past the lump in my throat to answer.

"I talked with your mom when I came in yesterday. Before I realized . . ." Her voice trailed off. "I hate to leave you here by yourself on Christmas. Do you want me to call someone for you?"

The nurse signaled through the glass. Lexi was waiting. "No thanks, I'll spend Christmas with Lexi . . . but will you come back?"

"Of course. Can I bring DaShawn?"

I nodded as the nurse came to wheel me into the NICU.

Thirty-nine

Shelley came back with DaShawn—the day after Christmas, and the day after that, and nearly every day until New Year's. I wasn't quite sure what to say to DaShawn, so I bought his eternal loyalty with Popsicles from the hospital fridge. When I asked about my job, Shelley said, "Don't worry about it, we'll get a temp to fill in for you. The job will be yours whenever you can come back." DaShawn brought his stuffed giraffe for Lexi, because he said, "I don't really need Raffe anymore."

Lexi made it through the first, critical forty-eight hours—with me sitting by her ventilator for most of them. Wrapped in wires and tubes, she looked like one of Kamran's cyborg sci-fi heroes. I used up another bar of cell-phone battery taking pictures of her and ran across the picture of stained-glass

Jesus. I forgot it was there, all this time.

"If she can make it through the first few days, she has an excellent chance," the NICU nurse told me. "And the more time you spend with her, the better she will do. When she's stabilized, you can hold her skin to skin."

Until then, I could stay by her side. They moved me out of Labor and Delivery and into Recovery, then to a tiny room with a cot down the hall from the NICU. "You can stay here until we need the room." A nurse gave me a tour of the area— a shower in the restroom, a coffee maker, a vending machine. After six months of chowing my weight in peanut butter, I couldn't bring myself to eat a bite.

I watched my daughter in the ventilator, where nothing could touch her but the wires and needles, taped to skin as thin as paper. She was even smaller than the giraffe I was holding—pink and mottled with hands like a doll's.

Xanda was a preemie, too. Had my parents been in my place, wondering if their baby would live or die? I couldn't picture it.

"You can talk to her," said my ob-gyn when she dropped by. "She knows your voice—she's been hearing you for months."

"What do I say?"

"Anything. Sing her a song. Tell her you love her. Tell her about your life. If you can't touch her skin, you can touch her with your voice."

I waited until we were alone in the ward, except for the occasional nurse scurrying past to check one of the monitors on the babies. The one in the jacket had jaundice, the light helping his body to process the excess bilirubin. Lexi's skin was still too delicate for the light jacket, too raw for even the lightest touch. Another had a huge hematoma on the back of her head, but at least she was fat and healthy.

The shaking baby was gone. I didn't know what happened to him.

Sing a song, the ob-gyn had said. She didn't know what she was asking for. I can't sing. Not in church, not onstage, not in an empty hospital wing with only an audience of infants. But the babies didn't care. They just needed a song.

I tried out the lines of Xanda's favorite Splashdown song. "'If they try to clip your wings . . .'" My voice cracked. The baby in the light jacket's chest raised and lowered, alone under the UV lamp. "'Fly away, far away,'" I sang again, "'I know why the caged bird sings.'"

Lexi lay there, maybe listening, maybe not. *Please God,* I thought as I breathed out another line of the song, *let her hear me. Maybe you can show me she's listening.* I watched for some sign from her, wrapped in all of those tubes and wires. An IV in her leg seemed thicker than her fingers. My leg ached, too, where the needle stuck out of her, getting in the way of my song.

"'I'll await my next escape to meet. . .'" The words stuck in my throat. "This is stupid. You can't hear me."

"'To meet with you again.'" I broke off, pressing my hands against the glass and willing her to feel them. "'You can't go, baby.'" The words escaped at little above a whisper.

This wasn't about Xanda anymore, whether or not the baby was her gift, or if she was the beginning or the end. Lexi hooked into my heart with tendrils like talons, tearing it out with every breath she couldn't take on her own.

I didn't know it would be like this.

In that moment, she stretched her neck, wrinkled like an elephant's trunk, and rolled her head toward me. The eyes, closed in tiny, lashless slits, opened—slightly at first, then all the way. Pupils, bright blue—the color of hope.

"Can you hear me?" I whispered. She blinked. Once, twice. Still looking, waiting for me to speak.

This labyrinth I had been traveling wasn't Xanda's—it was mine. My own daughter, who I thought was the bird to transport me away, wasn't the bird at all. She couldn't transport anyone, not even herself.

That was the beginning of my conversations with Lexi. As the jaundiced baby and the hematoma baby's parents came and went and new babies came through, I stayed with Lexi, quietly pouring out my heart. I drank coffee to keep myself awake, to keep myself talking. Singing. Telling her everything. By now the nurses knew better than to tell me to eat or rest. I couldn't tear myself away.

I took as many pictures as I could, until the battery on my cell phone went dead with the rhythmic vibration of seventeen messages waiting.

They brought a stack of board books. I couldn't read *Goodnight Moon*, or any of the good-night stories, for that matter. I focused on the love stories. *Guess How Much I Love You. The Runaway Bunny.* She was my bunny, trying to run away. But I wouldn't let her. Morning and night, I stood by her ventilator and touched the glass for days, for weeks, hoping she could feel my presence cradling her.

"Is it helping?" I demanded when the ob-gyn came to see me.

"Yes, it's helping. It's important just for her to know you are here." Her lips tightened. "You'll have to keep coming even now that you're discharged. You can stay as long as you like, except for during the nurse rounds and nights."

"Wait a second. You're kicking me out?"

She nodded grimly. "This is a busy hospital. You've been here for three weeks now, a lot longer than—"

I knew I couldn't camp out indefinitely. But now? "What about Lexi?"

"You can still use the parent facilities when you're here, and there's the waiting room." She picked up the copy of *The Runaway Bunny* and thumbed through the pages. "The nurses said your mom came by again."

"I don't care."

"I'm sure you could go home, if you wanted to." She opened to the page with the bunny on the tightrope wire. "Your mom cares about you, even if she doesn't know how to show it. Just like you care for that baby."

"She's nothing like me," I spat. "She would be happier if this baby died." *Wasn't she happier that Xanda died?*

"I'm sure that's not true."

But she didn't know what I knew. Andre didn't kill Xanda—she jumped. She pulled the door open, she jumped from a moving car. Maybe escaping to Hollywood wouldn't have been enough. Maybe she had to escape forever.

I watched Lexi in the ventilator, struggling in the tangle of threads keeping her tiny heart pumping. Every moment she lived meant another gram of hope.

She was going to live. We were both going to. And we were going to go where Xanda couldn't.

Forty

I spent the next couple of weeks living at the hospital like a homeless person—taking showers in the NICU bathroom, using hospital soap, wearing a hospital gown, pants, and robe and swapping them out whenever I could, using the shampoo left behind by other NICU parents. I slept in the NICU waiting room until the security guard started hounding me. Then I moved to Oncology, Cardiology, Urology . . . anywhere I could find an empty bench and a security guard out to lunch. Going home was not an option.

Coffee and Jell-O from the hospital fridge kept me from starving, plus whatever Shelley brought me when she visited—usually a bag full of pretzels, fruit roll-ups, and trail mix. She couldn't come into the NICU with me, but we could sit together at the window outside.

I had just come from a ketchup and cream cheese raid in the cafeteria when I heard a voice that could freeze my soul: "But I'm her grandmother!"

I stopped in my tracks and backed around the corner. As far as I knew, there was no alternate route to the NICU—my mother formed a wall between us. I peeked around the corner. I had a quarter view of her face—enough to see the tightness of her mouth and the judgment in her eyes. She wore her navy wool coat and clutched a paper bag brimming with clothes.

"I'm sorry, ma'am," a nurse was saying, "but you could be the president and we wouldn't be allowed to let you in without the parent's express permission. And she has asked for privacy." The nurse shook her head, brows downcast. "I really am very sorry. I wish there was something I could do."

"Well, there is. You can tell her—tell her, her mother . . . her mom came by to see her. And the baby. A girl? What's the baby's name?"

The nurse sighed. "Lexi," she said.

My mom's face turned white, jaw dropped. "As in, Alexandra?"

"I think so. But really, I'm not even supposed to give out that kind of information." The nurse began to turn away. "I'll tell her you were here."

"Thank you."

"But . . . you should keep trying. She might change her mind."

My mother huffed. I was already backing away, before she could storm right into me on her way to the elevator. I ducked into the restroom around the corner and locked myself in the farthest stall.

Seconds later, the door opened with a *whoosh*.

Damn.

Slam. She was in the first stall, yanking toilet paper out of the holder like Rapunzel's witch mother yanking on her hair.

"I don't believe this," she muttered, but the end of the sentence caught. All the things she used to say to Xanda echoed in my head: *dressed like a streetwalker . . . playing with fire . . . don't you see what you're doing to your life?*

I knew what I was doing, and Lexi would be with me.

Her door swung wide and crashed into the block of stalls, rattling the metal walls around me like a little earthquake. I imagined her peering through the half inch of space between the stalls with X-ray eyes—suspicious, hungry.

Instead, she went to the mirror. And what I saw was the last thing I expected.

The mask she wore, tightened and steeled against the world, slipped as she stared at herself. She blotted her eyes—rimmed red—with the wad of tissue and wiped the hair away from her face. She looked more than sad. She looked frightened, the same face I had seen on myself the day I came home last summer. Then the moment passed, making me question whether I had seen it at all. One final sniff, and she had disappeared behind that old door—NO UNAUTHORIZED ENTRY.

I stayed in the stall until my legs tingled, long after she was gone. But her presence was still in the room, a pair of eyes watching. I didn't dare look into the mirror as I rushed out of the bathroom. Who knew what eyes would be staring back at me.

Nik would show up in a few hours. Maybe by then I wouldn't be shaking.

She brought me a curried egg-salad sandwich from home. I scarfed it down while we looked through the window at Lexi. The baby had gained a pound since she had been born, going from a scrawny pink stick baby to a slightly less scrawny peachy one. Some days they put her in the light jacket to keep her from getting jaundiced.

"If it's not one thing, it's another," said Shelley. "She'll be like that for the rest of your life."

"You mean parenting?" I asked, rolling my eyes. Suddenly everyone had parenting advice for me.

"I mean the feeling that her life is out of your control." She smiled and patted me on the head, "Which is to say, yes. Parenting."

"I've been meaning to ask you something, actually," I said, taking another giant chomp of the sandwich. "Oooh, you brought chips, too. Thanks." I dove into the bag and crunched happily. I guess I was hungrier than I had realized.

"I just wondered . . . you've been coming here so much . . . is it bothering you to see Lexi and me? I mean, this has got to be painful. I don't know," I finished lamely.

But Shelley didn't grab the chips or take off running. Instead, she put her arm around me and squeezed my shoulders. "You've come a long way to ask that."

"What do you mean?"

"Well, I think you have to get to a certain place, get past your own needs to care about somebody else like that. So, thank you."

"You're welcome." I shrugged, loosening my grip on the chips. "What I wanted to ask, though . . . remember what you said about the future?"

"You mean when you were screaming?" She smiled.

"Yeah. Well, I wanted to know what you meant." All at once, everything juggling in my head for all these months came spilling out. I told her about Kamran's wormholes, and about the whys and hows of choices, hoping I managed to make sense.

"So what you said—about reasons being in the future," I finished in a jumble, "what did you mean?"

These were Nik kinds of questions. The kind you could ask someone who had lost something huge. A sister. Or a baby.

"Life is constantly weaving together, and we can look back and see all of the threads. Like your boyfriend's wormhole theory, except backward. We don't always know why things happen until down the road. That's what I meant."

My head was spinning like it did after Lexi came and I didn't have enough blood in my veins.

"Maybe she's going to die because I messed everything up.

Living with me would be a punishment anyway."

For the first time, Shelley looked like she might very well hit me. "Don't talk like that. Living is not a punishment."

"It takes a lot of faith to think like that."

"Yes, I suppose it does."

I was skeptical. Even though I wanted to believe what she was saying, to give some meaning to what happened to Xanda, what was happening to Lexi. "What about Micah James? Do you think you'll find some reason for him?"

I knew I sounded angry, and I was—for Xanda's death, the randomness of it, at Xanda for making the choice to jump out of the car, at my mother for driving Xanda away, at my father for introducing Andre to us. At the wrong turns I had taken, landing me without a sister, a friend, and a boyfriend and leaving me with a baby I wasn't even sure I could take care of, one that may or may not live. How could she talk about reasons?

"If something happened differently," I said, "maybe Micah James would still be here. Maybe Xanda would be, too. Why do these things happen?"

"I don't know. But I do know if it wasn't for Micah James, I might not be here with you."

Forty-one

Lexi went from the ventilator to the incubator, upgraded out of critical status. I could hold her close to my skin, tucked onto my chest, helping to stabilize her breathing, heart rate, and the strange twitches the nurses told me were common to premature babies who didn't yet have muscle control.

"Now that she can breathe on her own," said the pediatrician, "you're almost out of the woods. We're pleased with her progress so far. Another month, and she might be able to go home." Until then, the more I held her, the faster she grew. When I wasn't evading the hospital security guards or the nurse rounds, I spent a lot of time in the NICU rocking chair.

The day they declared Lexi could have visitors was the day Shelley brought cupcakes—plus her old "skinny" pants (still huge on me) and a couple of First Washington Credit Union T-shirts. Gold wasn't my color, but it was better than stolen hospital gowns. When I told her about my mom's visit, she said sometimes people's sadness looked like anger and judgment. What I didn't tell her about was the security guard finding me in an empty patient bed and chasing me all the way to the cafeteria.

On her eight-week birthday, Lexi was almost old enough to graduate from the hospital. The doctors were guessing another week, as long as she passed a critical series of tests. I dropped several hints to Shelley that brownies would be an excellent way to celebrate. More and more hours of the day were spent rocking Lexi, touching her skin tenderly and singing softly—every song I could think of, and when I couldn't think of any, I made them up. I was singing "Happy Birthday"—quietly and off key—when the nurse came into the room and said, "You have a visitor." I cuddled Lexi further into myself and sang, "Happy brownies for meeeee, happy brownies for meeeee."

"Wow," said a loud, familiar voice. "You look even worse than you sound."

I jerked in surprise, and Lexi jerked, too, snuffing and letting out a tiny mew. "Shhhh," I whispered in her ear and held her tighter, hoping she wouldn't be able to sense my heart racing. Her fist, the size of a cherry tomato, clutched my finger.

"Essence. What are you doing here?" I wouldn't have recognized her if it weren't for the voice, because she looked amazing, an echo of the face I used to know as well as my own sister's. Like the star she was becoming.

"I came because I heard the baby died."

"What?"

"That's what Delaney told everyone. She saw you pass out in a pool of blood and saved your life by calling nine-one-one."

And I suddenly felt like a sci-fi character, sucked back into the vortex of time and space and landing squarely back into my old life. "She would say that."

"You're not friends anymore?" She was such a good actor now, I almost missed the sarcasm.

"No," I said. "We're not friends anymore." I waited for the smirk, but it didn't come.

"Well, then you'll probably be happy to know she and Kamran are no longer an item. They broke up right after the Winter Ball."

"They did?" Lexi nestled further into my skin and raised her face toward me. Kamran's features echoed there—in the shape of her cheekbones, her head, her brow. "What happened?"

"He's not a complete jerk, apparently—he dumped Delaney after he saw her flip out on you at the dance. Then she transferred to Roosevelt."

On to reinvent herself again.

"That's what Kamran's telling everybody?"

"No. But that's what he told me. Right after you kicked him out of the hospital."

I couldn't believe she'd taken time out of her celebrity schedule to tell me all of this. Kamran and Essence were talking. Delaney was out of the picture. "I didn't kick him out," I said, not wanting to meet her eyes. At least half of the messages on my phone were from him, even though I never listened. "Well, not exactly."

"Geez, what is it about your family that nobody ever wants to tell the truth about anything?" She rummaged in her bag, pulling out a tiny pink knit hat with three butterflies embroidered on the front. "Here," she said, tossing it to me. "This is for the baby. I was supposed to tell you it's from me, but I'm sick of lying for everyone. It's from your mom. She's the one who told me you were here."

I dropped the hat into my lap. "So you're her messenger now. Of course you are."

"Oh, get over yourself, Rand. She saw the baby in the nursery and was worried about her head getting cold. So if you decide to get all huffy because it's from her, then whatever. It's a hat, not a pitchfork. And your mom isn't the devil. She cares a lot more about you than you give her credit for."

"And you know this because you've become her new best friend? Right after you stole my part in the montage?"

Essence's eyes narrowed. "Are you serious? I thought you never wanted to be on your mom's main stage again! You've been telling me that for how long now?"

I didn't say anything. She threw up her hands in exasperation.

"You don't get what you want, and you're not happy. You get what you want, and you're still not happy. You wouldn't even be happy if Xanda was still alive." The words stung more than if she had slapped me in the face. "You'd still be having problems with your mom, with or without your sister."

The baby in my arms was crying now, the cord between us severed but not entirely lost. I held her tightly, shushing her back into a state of peace. "That's enough! Enough."

"Sorry, I wasn't trying to upset you or the baby. But lately, or at least back when we were still friends, all I ever did was upset you. So I guess it's probably better we're *not* friends anymore."

"Don't say that, Essence."

"Why not?"

She was giving me a chance to apologize. For humiliating her in front of everyone at Milo's party. For choosing Delaney. For resenting when her life got better without me. For coveting the approval my mom gave her so readily now.

If I didn't, she would walk out that door and both of our lives would go on as they had, with regret scraping away at the edges of my heart even as I went on in my life with Lexi.

If I did, maybe the friendship we had wouldn't be lost. Nik would say it was a step of faith. Not knowing what the future would hold, but hoping somehow, somewhere, there was a plan for things to work out.

"Because . . . because I'm sorry." The tears came, and I didn't even bother trying to stop them. They came so easily, now that Lexi was born. "I'm sorry for everything. I don't want to not be friends anymore, Essence."

"That's a double negative. *And* a split infinitive." A half-smile pulled at her cheek. "But if that's your grammatically deficient excuse for an apology, then I will consider it."

I don't know why I thought she wouldn't. Essence had always cut me a lot of slack. Or maybe she knew I just wasn't used to blaming myself. It ran in the family.

"That doesn't mean you don't have to do some groveling. I realize you were under the spell of the Dazzling Delaney Pratt—"

"You mean the Despicable Delaney Pratt?"

"—the Depraved, Dreadful, Dangerous Delaney Pratt . . . but that doesn't mean you're off the hook." Her face went completely somber. "You were pretty mean to me this year."

I nodded. It was the truth.

"You made fun of me. You ditched me. You humiliated me. Then you blamed me for something I didn't even do. And you resented me for getting the stupid part you didn't even want."

Even worse, I had walked the path of Xanda's life alone, without the friend I needed most. I couldn't say anything to that.

"So I guess we'll have to see what happens. I don't know if I can trust you anymore."

I didn't know if I could trust myself.

"You should go home, Rand. Believe it or not, your mom misses you."

"Yeah, like she misses Xanda."

Essence gave me a penetrating look. "Maybe you should give her a chance. Things have changed . . . you should talk to her."

I wasn't so sure she would think so if I told her about my trip with Andre. Lexi made a snuffly sound, the signal she would want food soon. "But anyway," she continued, "I was hoping you'd let me see your baby. What's her name?"

If there was anyone in the world who would understand the connection, it was Essence. I fingered the safety-pin necklace around my neck and took a deep breath.

Then I told Xanda's story for the first time.

Forty-two

"Hey, what are you doing here?" a voice roared in my ear, dragging me up through a thousand layers of sleep. "I thought I told you not to hang around!"

The person in my face was huge. Angry. Spewing spit and breath that stank of old garlic. Steely eyes penetrated me like needles.

The security guard.

He wasn't supposed to be here. He had chased me out of a bed in the Gastroenterology wing, two floors down. Didn't he? Wasn't this Oncology? Didn't I have a few more days before I needed to find a new waiting room?

"Where's your patient I.D.? Who are you here to see?" He stood over me like a bulldog while I sat up, my heart pumping with adrenaline.

"I'm a patient," I stammered. "I was a patient. I mean . . ." I rummaged through my satchel.

He would let his guard down any second.

Fight or flight?

I wasn't even sure which I would choose until I found myself dashing over the other side of the bench and heading for the nearest stairwell, shaking off the sleep and clutching my satchel to my chest.

What floor was this again?

Footsteps thudded behind me in the corridor, empty in the early morning fluorescence. I glanced behind me to see my lead. He was heavy and muscular, like a wrestler, *thud thud thudding* in his boots. The sound echoed in the halls.

The door to the stairwell gave way under my weight. Something grabbed my First Washington Credit Union T-shirt—once gold, now a hazy yellow-gray—but it was only the handle, hooked around the hem.

Thud, thud, thud. "Hey, you come back here!"

Then the click of the door behind me muffled his voice.

I flew down the stairs two, three at a time, leaping to the bottom and struggling to direct my momentum to the next flight. He was in the stairwell, calling for backup on his walkie-talkie. *Teen, possible runaway. Headed down the south stairs.*

I hadn't run for months, but it came back to me in an instant. I was fast, faster than a middle-aged cop who'd eaten too many garlic bagels in the hospital cafeteria. I kept circling down, down the stairs, metal and gray and echoing my precise coordinates. I had to get out of here before someone caught me on the other end.

I burst out into an unfamiliar hallway, narrow and lined with rows of gray lockers, broken only by the occasional classroom door. The lights were low, the area deserted on a Sunday morning. I tried a few of the doors. Locked.

"Hey, stop right there!" The guard tripped, dropping his walkie-talkie. He went back for it, as well as for the battery that had skittered across the floor, buying me a few more seconds.

I nearly careened into an emergency shower in the hall, just in case I accidentally set myself on fire with hospital chemicals. My lungs were already on fire.

Past the elevator shaft, I found a second set of stairs and kept on running—through the corridors, winding and coiling like a serpent's tail into the very depths of the hospital. I stopped, tucking myself into an alcove, and listened.

Nothing.

I didn't know where I was, except I had reached the end of the line. Gigantic double doors barred my entrance with a sign, NO UNAUTHORIZED ENTRY in red and white, and a smaller sign reading, WARNING: FORMALDEHYDE IRRITANT AND POTENTIAL CANCER HAZARD.

I'd been here before, though something was off. The sign I'd seen before had a corner curled up from below, revealing a silver edge. Slowly, with my back in the alcove, I slid down the wall until I was the height of a twelve-year-old girl, crouching on the ground. The words loomed over me like they were ten feet tall.

And the corner, I realized with a chill. The corner curled up on the bottom edge, sharp and shiny as a razor. Exactly like the one I'd seen before, the night Xanda died.

Voices echoed down the hall—the security guard and someone else. "Maybe she went down this way." A grunt. Footsteps, coming my way. Which door was this?

There was no time to decide.

I tried the handle, slipped through, and closed the door with an airy thud.

The formaldehyde hit my nose first, bringing everything flooding back.

My eyes stung from the chemical, from the bright lights in this mostly metal room, lined with identical square drawers. The skin on my arms pricked with the cold, underscored by an electric hum. It was like the NICU, but vast and hollow, with a row of tables for full-sized people instead of babies.

One of the tables had a lumpy blue sheet, carefully laid out. Over a person.

A dead person.

A woman person, whose pale hair flowed out from under the sheet and dangled prettily off the edge. Her feet peeked out the other end, nails painted a jagged black, a tiny star tattoo twinkling on her toe. Like she was just sleeping, after a long party.

I would have cried out, but I could only gasp, and not even a full gasp, because the realization all but sucked the air out of me. A scream could summon the living and the dead.

Memory blurred into reality, like the razor's edge of the sign outside.

Everything was slipping out of my control.

I had to get out of here.

Footsteps pounded up to the other side of the door. "Think she went in here?" a new voice said—the other guard. Across the room, another exit sign signaled a stairwell, but there was no time. As the latch turned, I dove into a recessed corner.

Click. Swoosh. The guard poked his head into the room as I folded myself further.

"Nope, nobody in here," he called to the other guard. "Did you check the other corridor?" The door closed with an airy thud.

"I'll keep looking," said the other guard. "I hope she doesn't show up in here one of these days." Steps and voices faded away.

I slipped through another door and somehow found my way back to the NICU, as if Lexi had a homing beacon to draw me to her. When I reached the desk, Shelley sat there, waiting for me with a paper bag.

"I brought you a dress, just in case you wanted to go to church with me today. I know Lexi is going to be discharged in a few days, but I thought you might like to get outside."

"Church?" She had to be joking. I had just been to the depths of hell itself.

"Honey, are you all right? You look like you could faint dead away."

"Yeah," I mumbled, not meeting her eyes. "I'm fine." I had to be as pale as the body I'd seen. I put my hand over my nose, trying to wipe away the smell clinging to me like a shadow.

"Because if you—"

"Wait," I pleaded. "I have to ask you something. When Lexi can leave . . . when we can leave, can we live with you?"

Shelley's face transformed from smiling to something else, something I didn't want to see.

"We could ride to work together," I continued. "We could . . . eat curried egg-salad sandwiches together. I could take care of DaShawn when I'm not working—I still have the bank job, right?" I talked faster and faster as the adrenaline worked its way out of my system in a fevered rush.

She shook her head sadly.

The rush flooded into panic. "But why not? Things have been so great here! You could love Lexi, too. And you're like—well, not really like my mom anymore, you'd be more like a big sister. It would be like—"

"Rand. No."

Panic turned to tears, and I found I was running out of words. "But . . . why? Don't you care about us?"

Shelley sighed heavily. "Yes, I do. That's why you can't live with me. Even though it would be wonderful, and I would get to love Lexi, and DaShawn would be thrilled. But you would still be running away."

Damn it, why did I trust her? I could see my future crumbling, cracking open, and the floodwaters swallowing me up. "You're not listening," I accused.

"I have listened to every word you ever said, and even things you haven't said. You've been holing up here in the hospital for months now, feeling sorry for yourself and trying to make a future out of your past. You can't find yourself in other people, Rand. You can only be yourself. And you have someone right here in front of you who needs your whole heart, not just a piece of it while you're off looking for something else. A lot of people around you love you and want to love that baby, if you'd give them a chance. You've got to stop. You need to go home."

I couldn't believe what I was hearing. Home?

No, I wasn't going back there. And if my parents wanted to love Lexi, good. They could feel what it felt like to love someone and lose them. Maybe then they could take a good, hard look at themselves and see what they had done. And then they could be sorry. So, so sorry.

"Fine," I said, wishing I could say the hundred other angry words backed up like a simmering volcano. "Well, you should go to church. Confess, or whatever it is you do there. I've gotta go see Lexi now."

"We pray," she said quietly. "And we try to learn how to forgive."

When she was gone, I checked in with the nurses and grabbed my satchel. Nobody would be home on a Sunday morning. They would be off at church, praying for the sinners and hating the sin. I could hop a bus, run inside, and be gone before they said their last *Amen*.

Because as soon as Lexi was strong enough, we were out of here.

Forty-three

After Xanda stormed out on Christmas Eve with Andre in tow and her skirt still crackling in the fire, Mom patted her forehead. "I'm so glad that's over for the year. Mandy, get your things together so we can head to the church." As if it was all so . . . *normal*. I scrambled to get my boots and coat. Dad rolled his eyes and tossed a wad of wrapping paper into the fire, obliterating the skirt forever.

I felt like a defector, going with my parents after Xanda left, wearing the safety-pin necklace I gave her and not much else. She had squealed when she opened the little package from me. Delicately, she lifted the safety-pin chain out and held it up to the light.

"Look, Andre!" He draped across the couch like it was his

personal chaise. I knew Mom was angry at his cigarette smell, soaking into the fabric. We would hear about it later, even though she was glad that for once, Andre and Xanda were at our house instead of going *God knows where* and doing *God knows what.* He nodded. A nod of approval. "Rand made it for me. To go with my *dress.*" A giggle hiccupped on that last word. The sly smile spread across his face. I wished with all my heart that smile had been for me.

After they left, the memory of his smile lingered, so when I went onstage for the closing performance, I wasn't thinking of my mom's shouting or the skirt Xanda threw in the fire. I was thinking of his smile and nod of approval. I floated past the monstrous audience, all eyes pinning me to the sets my dad designed. I was only the girl in the white dress, lit up like an angel, or a white bird soaring out of the church and into the seat between my sister and Andre, where we would all fly away together.

My mother's choked gasp broke through my dream.

A murmur rose up in the crowd, and I was suddenly aware of the hundreds of dark heads watching me, listening, whispering among themselves. I heard my sister's name spoken in the crowd. If something had gone wrong, of course it had to do with her. The gossip, the snickering never stopped. *My poor mother. My poor father. And poor me, who had to follow in her footsteps.*

A police officer was standing backstage with my parents, speaking in a low voice.

My dad came out on the stage. Somehow he looked splintered, like the weight of our family had finally broken him. I looked to the wings, where my mother—her face a contradiction of red swelling and white angles—hissed, *"Don't."*

He started to speak. Haltingly, with deep cracks, the sound of pipes breaking through concrete. "Folks, there has been—"

In the split second before he could say "an accident," my mother's face transformed, anything vulnerable having been washed over by a clean hardness that could score glass. She was so beautiful, so formidable. And she strode out on the stage like a queen and smiled at the crowd, whose murmur had risen to a tight thrum of anxiety. She held out her hands for a ripple of calm. "Ladies and gentlemen," she announced, "we've had some technical difficulties, but our program will resume shortly. Please take a few minutes to get some cocoa in the lobby and enjoy the music while we get our act together." She said this last part with a chuckle.

The crowd visibly relaxed. Crisis averted. Still, I couldn't stop the panic flooding up through me. I inched my way closer to the wings where Dad stood, waiting for Mom.

He was not chuckling. He was crying.

And I started crying. Because a terrible fear had taken hold of me, to see my daddy cry and my mother crystallize into a diamond. She didn't even notice me standing there.

"Pull yourself together," she said in a low voice. "They need us to identify her."

I didn't even realize I was clutching my white dress in my hands, still standing on the stage with hundreds of people watching me. I couldn't stop the flood overtaking me, filling up my lungs and throat and eye sockets and spilling over and soaking into my white dress, or the sob escaping my lips. "What happened?"

All I could see was my daddy's red eyes, and my mother's tight face. I didn't hear how my voice had carried into the rafters of the church, echoing through the space and stopping everyone in their tracks. "Where's Xanda?" Everyone waited to hear the answer.

My mother enfolded me in her grasp, and I saw how a tear landed near my shoe and seeped into the wooden cracks of the stage. "Now look what you've done," she was saying to my father, all the while hugging me into her thin, cashmered body. My face scraped against the pearls around her neck.

"What *I've* done?" asked my father. He was gathering coats. Making himself useful. Ignoring the stagehands waiting to hear exactly what.

"This is all your doing, *Chuck*," she spat. "You hired him, you brought him into our house, you stood by and did nothing while he was out front . . . out front *screwing* our daughter." I felt my ears stinging, as if she had said the words to me. "And now . . ."

My dad stood, stunned, watching while she held me under her arm and steered me toward the back door. He meekly followed.

The words still echoed in my mind as I sat in the backseat of the car. They stayed with me when we disappeared into the white fortress of the hospital and traveled its corridors. They settled when they left me outside a door blaring NO UNAUTHORIZED ENTRY, where they went in as my parents and came out as people I didn't know at all.

Andre killed her. My dad killed her. My mother killed her. I wondered if somehow I had killed her, too.

Now, in the same hospital, Lexi had escaped death. She was days away from release.

Freedom.

I could be the bird to take us both away. All I had to do was pack a suitcase and go.

Forty-four

The bus wound through the hills of our neighborhood as I made a mental list of everything I would need: money, food, clothes, cell phone charger. All of it would have to fit in Dad's camping duffle bag, still stashed in the laundry room.

I would have to clean out my bank account, just in case they started looking for me. After saving every penny from my job, I had enough to keep us in diapers and milk for a while. Then there was Dad's quarter collection, the bond from Uncle Brit, and the pearl necklace Mom's parents gave me for my seventeenth birthday. Hard to believe it was nearly a year ago.

There was so much I would have to leave behind—drawings, photos, letters. I touched the safety-pin necklace around my neck, wishing I could take the dress. If I had time, I could plop my portfolio onto a disk so I'd at least have *something* to show when I looked for a job. Painting movie sets? Coloring sci-fi eyes? Whatever I could do that would keep Lexi and me afloat. If we could get there, find someplace to sleep, I could figure the rest out later.

I asked the bus driver the time. Eight forty-three. Perfect—they would have just left for church, giving me a good three hours.

Our house looked the same, but infinitely different. Same driveway, same car, same door, same windows, same bars. I wondered if my key would work.

It did.

When I caught a glimpse of the foyer mirror, I barely recognized the pale, haunted person I saw, except for the eyes—like Xanda's, Mom's, and now Lexi's. If only I could find another path, Lexi would be different.

I hurried to find the duffle bag.

The carpet on the stairs felt familiar under my feet, though the art on the walls had changed completely. My drawings, gone. Erased. Just like Xanda.

My door stood closed and Xanda's room—the office—was open a crack. My bedroom was exactly as I'd left it: maternity clothes draped over the chair, shoes cluttered in the bottom of the closet, books stacked on the desk next to a binder full of class notes. Here was life before Lexi, splayed out like that corpse.

Everything looked the same, except for a small, pink bundle

placed neatly on the bed. A package of fluffy pink baby sleepers. As if that was supposed to make up for everything.

I stuffed them into the duffle bag and got to work—underwear, jeans, hoodie. A dress, for interviews. A blanket, for Lexi. I'd have to get her some real clothes, and diapers. I plugged in my phone and it blinked to life. Carefully, I gathered the photos from my bulletin board—me and Essence. Me and Kamran. I would call him once we got there, if he would still talk to me. Maybe his parents would like to know they had a grandchild.

I surveyed my room one last time, the briefest of good-byes to my old life.

Next stop: the office, where I would transfer my files and erase my electronic existence. I'd be giving my parents a head start.

The office would always be Xanda's bedroom to me, no matter how the furniture was arranged. Her purple walls had been painted a nice celery green, to draw attention to the view. But when I stood in the doorway, I wasn't taking in the view.

Instead, I took in the hundreds of photographs spread across the floor, the couch, the desk—pictures traveling the length and breadth of the Mathison family. Photographs I thought my mother had destroyed. Every one of them was a window, a chronicle of lost time and space.

I went into the room and picked them up one by one—Mom and Dad, about my age, holding up a squashed, purple baby who looked exactly like Lexi, only bigger. Mom and

Xanda the toddler, playing tea party. Xanda as a little girl, missing her two front teeth and clutching a baby, perilously balanced on her spindly knee. Me, looking half delighted and half terrified.

Someone sniffled behind me.

My mother stood in the doorway in her robe, eyes red and puffy and hair gathered into a loose ponytail. "What are you doing here?"

There would be no disk now.

I knew what I looked like to her—hair ratted, swimming in this yellow First Washington T-shirt, getting my fingerprints all over her secret stash. The duffle bag lay open next to me, clothes and sketchbook stuffed inside.

"I came to get a few things."

Mom's eyes sealed up.

"Going to stay with your dad?"

I gave her a blank look. "Dad's gone?"

She shrugged. "He left. Cleared a few things out while I was at opening night and you were running around Seattle."

"I was hospitalized!"

"Not on my watch. You left my car. You got out, just like—"

She stopped. Her eyes fell on the picture I held in my hand. I remembered when it was taken—when we'd all taken a car trip down the coast and Xanda had disappeared into the redwoods at the Trees of Mystery with some boy, and when she'd come out a half hour later, Mom had come unglued. *We thought somebody grabbed you. If you ever do anything like that again, Dad's going to chain you up in the trunk, understand?* But before she'd disappeared, someone had shot a picture of the four of us, smiling, on Paul Bunyan's ginormous shoe. I'd forgotten that picture existed.

"Mom, I know what happened to her."

"Andre," she spat. "I saw you with him. If it wasn't for that boy—"

"Stop blaming Andre! Stop blaming Dad!"

We both jumped at the sound of my voice.

Her eyes narrowed. "I don't know how you think you can judge me. You've spent the last year doing everything possible to decimate your life and head down the same path as your sister. You have no idea what you're talking about."

My baby had spent the last three months in the hospital, her life dangling by a thread while everyone looked to me, the teenage train wreck. I had every idea.

"And you have no idea," she continued, much more softly now, "what it's like . . ." She broke off, not willing—or maybe able—to finish the sentence.

Instead, she took up one of the photos—the one of her and dad in the hospital with baby Xanda. I knew where this was going. Xanda was the preemie, the reason we were all here now.

"That was the day your sister was born," she said. Seven months after the wedding, as my mom's parents were quick to note. Xanda peeked out of the blanket like she was already sizing up the world. If anyone could survive preemiehood, it was her.

"But she looks huge," I gasped, and Mom frowned. Where was the IV? "She looks so . . . healthy, for a preemie." I thought of Lexi, fighting her way out of the tubes and wires in order to come home. Only two pounds at birth, now up to a fighting weight of just over five.

Mom bent over the pictures until her hair covered her face and her shoulders bounced, hugging herself to keep from bursting. Laughing. At me? At Lexi?

"What?" I snapped. I didn't have time for this. I had a bus to catch.

She put her hand on my arm, about to tell me where I could go. I'd tell her I didn't care anymore about her judgment. She could heap coals of fire, and they wouldn't even touch me. I had Lexi now.

I looked at the photo again, and I realized I'd never seen it before. *Seven months after the wedding.* And Xanda looking as fat and healthy as the hematoma baby, who could have eaten Lexi for a snack.

You know—rich girl and the construction guy, Andre had said.

Xanda wasn't a preemie. She never was.

"You were pregnant when you got married? Pregnant with Xanda?"

Mom's hair parted as she nodded. And I could see all at once that the mask of her face, always seeming too tight, covered a vast sorrow—maybe even as vast as my labyrinth—and a terrible secret. The blame she doled out so easily grafted over a deeper, quieter voice.

Shame.

"I've been . . . I haven't felt like myself for a long time, wondering what I did or didn't do, what I could have done to change what happened to your sister. I wanted to do better with you." I thought of Shelley in the hospital, how she said sometimes sadness only looked like anger and judgment. Maybe fear did, too.

Her eyes met mine. "Do you think it was my fault she died?"

If someone had asked me yesterday or even ten minutes ago, I would have known the answer. But now I wasn't so sure.

My thoughts raced back through the tangle of events to the moment of *why*. It was easiest to blame my mom for Xanda's death and everything that had happened since, because then I'd never have to look too closely at myself. At what I had done to Essence. Kamran. Shelley. Blaming Essence for what happened to our friendship. Using Kamran and then Shelley as a means of escape. *Maybe you think this baby is going to make up for everything*, Delaney had said.

Was I doing the same to Lexi? Would my choices now affect the pattern of her future?

My breath caught as the thought sunk in. I thought of the time Xanda let me try on her safety-pin ensemble. "You don't want to be like me," she said. "You'd be better off being like Mom than me." I had spent so long trying to act like Xanda that I didn't notice myself acting like Mom—feeling shame and blaming everyone else.

Mom's question still hung in the air, and I thought of the last thing Shelley said. *We try to learn to forgive.* Blame was not forgiving other people. Shame was not forgiving yourself. We each had a little of both.

"No," I said. "I don't think it's your fault." It felt like a part of me flew up into the sky and away like the bird in my drawing—the part carrying around a weight for a long, long time.

"But it is. Xanda died, your father left, you . . ." She didn't finish, but I knew she was going to say something about Lexi.

"Lexi isn't a punishment," I said gently. "If you could see her . . ." My duffle bag lay in my lap, sketchbook tumbled at an angle. In the hospital, I'd drawn Lexi over and over until her face was as natural to my pencil as labyrinths had ever been. "I took pictures. And . . . I could show you my drawings."

"Lexi," my mom echoed. I held my breath, waiting for her to pass judgment. "It's beautiful." Another part of me took flight, the one waiting to hear those words.

As we looked at the drawings together, she held her breath, too—first at the tiny creature dwarfed by the blankets and monitors, then as she grew each week. The only labyrinths were the tubes and cords, which gradually disappeared as she made huge steps toward self-sufficiency. In the last one, she wore the pink hat Essence brought from my mom, her head swamped in the soft cotton and her eyes bright.

"I know why you did what you did," my mom said softly. "I wouldn't have given Xanda up, either." She sighed as she looked over the photos and picked up the one of her and Dad at the hospital with baby Xanda. "You probably won't believe this, but everything I've done, I did because I was trying to protect you and your sister—from making the mistakes I made. Maybe you can understand, after what you've been through. Andre is so much like . . ."

"Like Dad? Mom, you act like he's spent the last fifteen years drinking beer on the couch instead of working so hard for all of us. Don't you see who he is? He's not *Chuck*. Chuck doesn't even exist."

Mom nodded, her eyes shining. "It's funny. I didn't think your dad would be the one to do the leaving. But now that he's gone . . ." She sniffed, shaking her head. "I just . . . didn't think I would miss him this much."

"You have to talk to him." Even as I said it, I felt a pang of guilt about Kamran. I hadn't been fair. I hadn't talked to him about anything, especially about what was most important. Even if it was wrong, I could understand why he'd broken up with me. Just like Dad did to Mom. Was it even possible to make things right?

Mom nodded. "Things have been so different, since . . ." She paused, looking to me before continuing. "Since Xanda died. I don't know how it will go."

I closed my sketchbook. "Maybe you can tell him what you told me." Maybe there was a chance to start over—with Lexi. I knew forgiveness wouldn't be simple, but if anyone could help us with it, she could.

I picked up one picture, then another, and Mom joined in. Together we gathered the scattered threads of our lives.

Forty-five

I became an older sister the day I turned eighteen.

It felt strange to finally leave Xanda behind, frozen in memories and photographs. After we sorted pictures in the office, Mom and I framed and hung them in the stairwell— Xanda, me, my parents, our friends, and she added more of Lexi every day. Is this what forgiveness looked like? I didn't have much time to think about it, with Lexi crying on one side and Mom making suggestions on the other.

"You'd better hurry up—your dad's going to pick you up any minute for the Cornish tour."

I assessed my reflection in the bedroom mirror. Totally sleep deprived. Too thin for my skinniest jeans after staying up with Lexi and running on nothing but fingernails and adrenaline, wearing Xanda's fuzzy red sweater in an attempt to look like a serious student. I didn't have to try too hard. I already looked like I'd lived a whole life.

I shifted my satchel away from my stomach, still not quite used to being only myself. Sometimes I even felt a phantom baby kicking as I was falling asleep—a notion that burst the second I heard Lexi's snuffling through the darkness, a cry holding the power of a thousand tiny electrical currents connected to my nervous system. In all the fantasies I had about Lexi before she was born, the connection between us now—invisible and excruciating—never crossed my mind. That, or the way she would have no sense of time, if she should be asleep or awake at any given hour. Especially at night.

"It's all par for parenthood, Miranda," Mom would say. "It's what you signed up for, remember?" Smug. But not so smug that she didn't give me two seconds of sympathy and maybe even pancakes after a particularly long, wakeful night.

Things had been difficult in the hospital, but bringing Lexi home was something else altogether: putting her on a strict two-hour feeding schedule to keep her from losing precious ounces; monitoring her for signs of jaundice; listening to her breathing, waiting for the skipped gasp that would send us back to the NICU.

In the hospital, I'd had help. At home, it was all me.

"At least you're young and can handle a few all-nighters," Mom had joked. After ten or twelve all-nighters, though, it got considerably less funny. After a month, it came across as simply hostile. Then she would shock me by following up with a brief, stiff hug and, "Why don't you go take a nap? I can watch the baby for a while."

Not that this perpetual state of awakeness would change my feelings about Lexi. You know you love someone when you willingly give up that much sleep for them.

Dad arrived a few minutes later in his beat-up construction truck to take me on a tour of Cornish College of the Arts.

He and Mom still had a lot to work out, but at least they were trying. She was trying, especially—reaching out where she hadn't before. Taking on responsibility as forgiveness moved in. Looking in corners that, after lying unnoticed for the five years since Xanda died, needed serious spring cleaning. Luckily, Mom hated dirt. And she loved my dad, more than she'd realized, I guess. Enough to look into the darkest corners of her own heart.

"Here, take this," Mom said, handing me a peanut butter and jelly sandwich. She straightened my sweater and brushed off a fleck of lint. Then she sighed. "Good luck," she said, giving me a quick squeeze.

It was one of those rare April days where the sun came out of hiding and shone brilliantly on Seattle and the surrounding lakes.

"Don't worry," Mom called from the front door with Lexi tucked into her arm like a football, "I'll take good care of the baby."

That lasted about five minutes—enough time for me to get

into the truck, up the hill, and into my own personal panic attack. What if something happened while I was gone?

Dad gave me a knowing smile and turned the truck around. I knew what that smile said. *Sometimes you're just like your mother.* But I was glad he didn't say it.

After we'd swapped cars, packed the diaper bag, and got a wailing Lexi fastened into the car seat, we were on our way.

Cornish itself looked like a medieval castle on one of the highest hills in the city, with Lake Union and downtown on one side and a network of neighborhoods—including ours—on the other. In the unexpected brightness of the sun, we could see it all, churning, winding, and sparkling.

We escaped the crisp air through a pair of great, ancient doors and into a maze of halls leading in every direction. I could see exactly why Essence wanted to come here and why she thought I should, too. It was like one big drama class. Everyone bustled through the tunnels, their talking and laughter bouncing off the walls. Individuals headed off to sketch or journal in the garden while groups sprawled in the common spaces.

"This is an amazing place," the student at the info desk told me as he handed over a stack of papers. "When you come here—well, I can tell you, it will change your life."

My life had already changed so much, and it was still changing in drastic, immeasurable ways.

When I had dialed Kamran's cell phone a few weeks before, he'd picked up halfway through the first ring.

"Miranda," he said. "I've been waiting for you." And it was like all the time and space between us, over these whole last nine months, compressed into one moment—not of perfection, but of something sweet and familiar and real.

"I'm sorry I didn't call," I said, the words tripping over themselves. There was so much more. Like Essence pointed out, no one in my family told the truth about anything. Maybe it was time for me to start.

He picked up Lexi and me with his parents' car. I strapped Lexi into the back, where the leather upholstery smelled clean and new, with a hint of his dad's sandalwood aftershave. Kamran watched from a distance, as if somehow his proximity could shatter her. I knew better. However delicate she looked on the outside, inside she was stronger than wire.

"We should go for a walk," he said. "Talk about things." The future, with him on one end of the country and me on the other. What was there to talk about?

He parked near the University Bridge, and we struck out on the Burke-Gilman Trail, a footpath sweeping past the university and along Lake Washington. We were close, not touching, reminding me of the *pat pat pat* he had given me when we first saw each other last fall. Neither of us wanted to be the first to speak.

Lexi protested when I tucked her into the front pack, then quieted with the rhythm of my steps. The University of Washington loomed ahead, bright in the March light, with the path rolling out before us.

We stopped at a bench under the astronomy building with

the sundial clinging to the outside of it like a copper-green spiderweb, a lazy figure eight marking months and minutes, patterns of time.

"There's a reason I brought you here," Kamran began, looking as though he might have to spring any second to catch Lexi if she slipped out of the carrier. Beneath her, my heart thudded, waiting for the words to tumble out of his mouth. "I'm not going to MIT."

I sat there beside him, letting it sink in. "Not going?"

"I didn't get in. Too focused. Or not focused enough. The letter didn't really go into it."

"But . . . what about . . ."

"Harvard? Well, that's what I wanted to talk with you about. I'll be here, at the U." He glanced up at the sundial. "I got into the Aeronautics and Astronautics program. After MIT, it's one of the best in the country, plus there's a scholarship, so . . . I'll be around, is what I'm trying to say."

In an instant, everything had changed, yet again. "I'm going to Cornish," I said.

"I know."

"Essence," we both said at the same time. He smiled, that smile that had captured me yesterday, today, and the days to come—not because it was like Andre, but because it was his very own.

"So . . . I've been thinking," he was saying. "I've been doing a lot of thinking. And . . . we'll both be here . . ." His knee bounced up and down the way it did when he was worried.

". . . and I was thinking maybe you were right, maybe we should—"

Here he was, about to say the words I had always hoped to hear. And yet, it was all wrong—the right words spoken at the wrong time, in the wrong place, in the wake of all the wrong reasons. There was nothing else I could say but, "No."

"No?" He blinked, a quick kiss of lashes.

"No." My voice felt stronger, more solid. When he looked puzzled, I closed my eyes. What would Xanda say? I didn't know. I only knew what I had to say.

On the bench under the sundial, I told him what I'd wanted to tell him the night of the Winter Ball: that in him, I'd been looking for the door to unlock my sister's life, that I'd made him into someone else's image, and most of all, that I was sorry.

Since that day at the university, he'd already been over to the house a few times—getting to know Lexi, and getting to know my parents. I was getting to know him—the real him, not what I wanted him to be.

"He's a good kid," my mom said, after he tried teaching her how to make lamb kebabs while I gave Lexi a bath in the kitchen sink. At first he was nervous, but now he held Lexi all the time.

Here, at Cornish, Lexi snuffled and fussed, signaling imminent meltdown. I looked over at my dad, who seemed to be waiting for me to decide what to do.

"Thanks," I said to the student at the info desk, dashing out the front doors with my dad close behind.

The air smacked us, but in the way that makes you feel like it's just been cleaned by a good, hard storm. Lexi's crying gained momentum in the wide-open space while I bounced, swayed, shushed, anything I could to get her to quiet down for the tour.

"It's too bad your mom didn't come with us," said my dad—still uncomfortable in his new roles. Father, revisited. Husband in revision. Grandfather in training.

"It's okay," I said, though I was anything but sure as I continued to bounce. "I can handle it. Besides, she's probably writing notes for next year's montage." It was going to be different this year, she promised. "I won't even ask you to be in it," she said in an uncharacteristic flash of shyness, "unless you want to. You and Essence. And Lexi." I wondered what part she'd already dreamed up for Lexi—only my mom could get away with giving baby Jesus a gender change.

My bouncing wasn't working. "I'm going to try walking instead," I said, and we headed for the garden.

"It's time for the big college tour," I sang, but Lexi clearly wasn't listening, unless she was listening to the sound of her own impressive pipes.

Maybe this tour hadn't been such a great idea. I switched to a sway, sway, sway that I hoped would rock her back to sleep. I could see myself sway, sway, swaying through class, at the easel, handing in my portfolio, getting my diploma . . . all the while swaying to keep Lexi from having a small eruption.

A couple of girls walked past, giggling and sharing a look at a magenta cell phone, slinging their messenger bags with their hips as they walked. I could have been one of them, I thought, if I had made some other choice. They cooed at the baby as they walked past.

Without the pregnancy to keep me warm, I had to pull my jacket and scarf closer around the two of us. Dad put his arm around me. Across the sound, the Olympic Mountains—a force risen out of the depths—now rested under a layer of clean, white snow. "I don't say it much, Miranda, but I thought you should know I'm really proud of you. It's a hard thing to protect what you love. Sometimes you can't. But it's a good thing when you try. I know Xanda would be proud, too."

"Thanks, Dad." I hugged him back. The future was going to be difficult—I was still catching up with school in time to graduate, not to mention slowly repairing my friendship with Essence and figuring things out with Kamran.

But maybe that wasn't such a bad thing. Because now we had Lexi.

"We'd better go in for the tour," Dad said, steering me gently toward the double doors—complete with stained glass, shimmering with shadows and light. A stream of bodies rushed from one class to another, worlds unfolding in front of them in this castle of crossed destinies. I stood on the threshold. It was hard to imagine myself knowing where to go without Xanda going before me.

Would we really be able to do this?

It's the grit that makes the pearl, Shelley said when I called, right before she offered me my old job back. She'd even stopped by a couple of times, just to visit.

I started to sway Lexi again when I realized she was quiet. Waiting. Both of us paused on the cusp of the unknown. I couldn't go backward or even retrace my own steps, let alone Xanda's. I could only go forward. The threads of time weren't unraveling but weaving into a tapestry—a future, and a hope.

The only way to discover was to step into it.